The Illest Taboo 2

(An Enemies to Lovers Romance)

by

K.L. Hall

This book is a work of fiction. Names, characters, places and incidents are either the product of the author's imagination or are used fictionally. Any resemblance to actual persons, living or dead, or to actual events or locales is entirely coincidental.

the illest taboo 2 synopsis.

ta·boo: *a forbidden association with a particular person, place, or thing.*

No matter how hard she tried, River's resolve to stay away was no match for the East Atlanta bad boy with tattoos and a rap sheet as long as his paper. Now that an unexpected arrest has left her relationship with Mav hanging in the balance, River begins to question her best friend's past and Mav's role in her demise. How much did she really know about her best friend, and what would she do if the man she loved actually killed her? When she learns the truth, River is left to decide if she can love the light and dark sides of everything that is Maverick Malone.

When news of his arrest for Luca's murder ignites the streets of Atlanta, Mav knows whoever set him up just made the price on his head even greater. With one foot already out of the game, he recognizes that going legit won't buy his soul back from the streets. Mav finds himself torn between self-preservation and avenging his blood. The streets are calling, but so is River's heart. Can he prove himself to be the man she needs, or will he choose himself in the end? Once loose ends are tied, claiming checkmate and divorcing the game is the *only* goal.

In this series finale, hearts will be surrendered, lives will be lost, and breaking points will be shattered. Will the love between River and Mav prove to be true, or will they decide that the risk simply isn't worth the reward?

author acknowledgments.

Gracias. Merci. Grazie. Mahalo.

If you're reading this right now, thank you.

Always,

K.L. Hall

epigraph.

"I knew I did from that first moment we met.
It was...not love at first sight exactly,
but—familiarity. Like, oh, hello, it's you.
It's going to be you.
Game over."

-Mhairi McFarlane

Previously in The Illest Taboo…

Mav

I let out an irritated sigh and walked into the kitchen. She followed behind me as I leaned forward, my fingers laced before me on the countertop. "Tek was able to unlock the phone, so I picked it up earlier," I told her.

"Did you go through it?"

"Yeah, I did."

"And? What was on it?"

"See for yourself," I said, pulling it out of my back pocket and handed it to her.

She took the phone. "What exactly am I supposed to be looking at?"

"Proof that their car accident wasn't an accident, River. My brother and Suki were murdered."

Her hands shook as she looked through the phone. "W—what is all of this, Mav? What the fuck was Suki into?"

My lips parted, but before sound could come out, the doorbell rang. I shot my eyes to River and then made my way to the door.

"Maverick Malone?" a white police officer asked.

I grimaced. "Who wants to know?"

"You are under arrest for the murder of Luca and Suki Malone. You have the right to remain silent. Anything you say can and will be used against you in the court of law..."

Prologue

It was raining out. Pouring, even. Old mothafuckas would say it was raining cats and dogs. I sat posted in my truck across the street and watched as the valet brought their car around. They stood hand-in-hand, giggling like a couple of teenagers without a care in the world. He even took his jacket off and gave it to her to protect her hair from the rain. A true fuckin' gentleman.

I waited until she got in the passenger seat, and he pulled off, keeping my distance for a few lights before tailing them closer and closer. The downpour continued to cascade down my windshield as my wipers swiped vigorously back and forth, trying to clear my sightline of the road ahead. The engine revved as I pressed harder on the gas, ready to let them know they were being followed. The closer I got, the faster he sped, trying to put enough distance between us so that I'd either get caught up by a light or the police, whichever came first. What happened next was unexpected. I was riding his bumper so hard that he ran the red light and was struck by an oncoming SUV right on the driver's side.

SMACK!

My tires screeched as my truck fishtailed against the wet pavement. I gripped the wheel tighter as my brakes grinded to a halt. The violent thudding of my heart was enough to make me pass out as I tried to catch my breath. Jumping out of my vehicle, I wasted no time running over to the car that had gone from a luxury vehicle to a crumpled piece of metal in seconds. Glass was fractured into a million pieces across the slick pavement as I yanked open the passenger side door and unhooked her seatbelt to pull her out.

"Are you okay?" I asked, cradling her battered body in my arms.

I glanced over at her man who was laying slump against the deployed airbag with blood leaking from his head. He didn't stand a chance.

She blinked slowly, unaware of what had just happened. After a few seconds of panicked fast breaths, she locked eyes with me. "You..." she whispered.

Her disoriented body stiffened in my arms, and I gifted her a devilish grin. "I told you what would happen if you kept fuckin' with me, didn't I? Now, where the fuck is my money?"

"P—please," she pleaded.

She was weak and battered, but I didn't give a fuck. She'd wronged me like no other woman had ever done before, and she was going to pay one way or another. "Please, what? Huh? It's too late to beg now, you fuckin' bitch. Tell me what the fuck you did with my money!" I yelled, jabbing my gloved fist into the side of her face.

Her once beautiful face shattered like a fragile piece of glass beneath my rage. She screamed out in pain as her neck flung backwards.

"You've got one more time to tell me where the fuck my money is, or I'm gonna put the period at the end of this sentence," I warned, before jabbing her again.

Bitches like her didn't like to listen. She needed tough love. She screamed out again and again, saying my name, begging for forgiveness in her utmost moment of need. I wanted to hear her scream louder, like she did each and every time we fucked. For the past eight months, Suki had prided herself on having me wrapped around her little diamond-encrusted finger. Anything she wanted, I supplied until I found out the details of our whirlwind romance weren't nearly as important to her as they were to me. I expected her to get with the winning team and leave her husband for me, not butter me up so that she could rob me blind. Her actions had proven that she was nothing but a selfish bitch who thought she could have her cake and eat it too. As a result, she had to learn the hard way not to write a check her pretty ass couldn't afford to cash. She truly didn't know who she was fuckin' with.

"What did you do with my money!" I raged, shaking her shoulders.

Fading in and out of consciousness, Suki extended her tongue, tasting the zest of fresh blood on her lips. With the last bit of strength she had left in her, she sliced her nails down the side of my face. "Kiss that money goodbye," she whispered.

I sucked my teeth. Even in her last moments, she was going to go out like a G. There was a slight part of me that respected it, but not enough to let her live. I didn't have any other choice in the matter. "That's a shame. You should've chose up, baby girl. I could've given you everything, Suki! Everything!"

A single tear slipped down her face, mixing seamlessly with the falling rain. "P—please, I—I..."

"All you had to do was keep it real with me. We had a good thing, right? You were supposed to leave this nigga for me! And yet you decided to break my heart and steal from me. And what did I tell you would happen if you ever

lied to me, huh? I told you you'd pay, didn't I? Didn't I?" I asked, enveloping my gloved hands around her throat.

"I—I'm pregnant! And... it's yours..." she revealed, her tear-stained eyes helping to plead her case.

I paused and looked her deep in her eyes. She was the type to say anything to get out of dying, but I'd seen the test she buried at the bottom of my trashcan three weeks ago with my own two eyes. She was telling the truth and waited for the last possible moment to play the only card she had left. My grip tightened once more as I pulled her lips close to mine. Her breathing was shallow, signaling that her last breath was only a heartbeat away. "I know," I whispered.

Feeling her throat shatter and collapse between my hands was priceless. I stepped over the broken glass and tossed her lifeless body back inside the car before planting drugs and liquor inside the vehicle. Even through all the smoke and steam from the crash, I could see the strobe of police lights in the distance.

"I'm sorry it had to end this way, but you never should've fuckin' crossed me," I mumbled before jumping back into my truck and leaving the scene.

Mav

"You have the right to remain silent. Anything you say can and will be used against you in a court of law. You have the right to an attorney..."

I'd fully zoned out.

I'd had my "rights" read to me what felt like a hundred times. I knew the drill. I glued my eyes to River's as the cold handcuffs confined my wrists. I searched for comfort, and all that stared back at me was fear.

"What the hell is going on? Why are you cuffing

him? He didn't do anything wrong!" River yelled before helplessly pressing her heart-shaped lips together.

I could tell by the distant look on her face and the glossy haze over her eyes that she was completely devastated over the entire thing. The sight of tears sliding down her round face made my knuckles tense up and set my throat on fire. I hated seeing my baby like that. It was enough to make me want to break out of the cuffs and kill everybody in my way just so I could catch them before they fell. All I ever wanted to do was make her smile and do anything to wipe away the pain she was feeling.

"I'm going to get out, don't worry. Everything is gon' be fine, I fuckin' promise!" I yelled out to her.

I stared, refusing to tear my eyes away from her even when they pushed me into the back of the dirty ass police car. I wanted to capture everything about her, even if she wasn't at her best. Her hair was in a high messy bun with loose ringlets of her natural curls swinging at the nape of her neck. There were small beads of sweat populating on her forehead as terror sparkled in her cedar brown eyes. She dug her nails into her clover honey colored skin, screaming, crying out to deaf ears with twisted lips and a crinkled nose. When the car pulled off, all I could do was pray too much time didn't pass until I saw her again.

WHEN I GOT to the jail, I made my phone call. Little did they know, I had a lawyer on payroll. Joel Weinberg was one of five partners at Weinberg and

Associates, and he was a fuckin' shark.

"Hello?" he answered.

"Get down to the precinct. They got me fucked-up out here, tryna pin Luca's death on me."

"What? Okay, okay. Sit tight. I'll be down there soon."

"Call Sosa and tell him to check on the house. He'll know what I mean."

"Got it."

I hung up the phone, knowing whoever put the target on my back was honing in slowly but surely. Niggas would always show me respect in jail, but I could never be sure if someone would try something. At that point, everybody was lookin' like an enemy to me, and I needed to talk to Sosa. He was the only person outside of myself I could trust to help me get to the bottom of who'd killed my brother, and why they thought they had the power to set me up to take the fall for it.

They put me in a holding cell with nothing but four concrete walls and a door with a rectangular cut out for a window. I propped my foot up against the leg of the steel table just as two investigators in cheap ass suits walked in.

"How ya doin', Maverick? That's a cool name, huh,

Pratt," one said, elbowing his female partner in the side.

"Sure is, Wilson," she nodded, "but listen, Mav. Can I call you Mav? We just want to chat, that's all."

"I ain't got nothin' to say."

"Oh, sure you do," Wilson said, leaning in to me. "Let's start with you telling us where you were the night your brother was killed."

The smell of old coffee and cigarette butts on his breath churned my stomach. "I don't have to tell you shit because I ain't do shit, but somethin' tells me you already know that."

Pratt folded her arms. "If you're innocent, then what's the harm in telling us where you were that night? If your story checks out, you have nothing to worry about."

I cut my eyes at her and shrugged. "I ain't worried now. We both know if y'all had shit, there would be no need to talk. You're just trying to buy time before my lawyer gets here."

"Listen, the faster you cooperate with me, the easier this will be for everybody. So, I'll ask you again, where were you the night of the accident?" Wilson interjected.

"You really wanna know where I was?" I asked, adjusting my position in the hard plastic chair.

“Yeah.” He nodded.

“I was in the crib gettin’ topped off by your bitch.” I smirked. I wouldn’t give them the satisfaction of seeing see me sweat.

“Oh, I see we got a real clever mothafucka on our hands, huh?” Wilson retorted.

Pratt nodded, pulling her dark brown hair into a ponytail. “Not clever enough though…looks like cell phone towers pinged your number not too far away from the scene of the accident that night. Can you explain that?”

Before I had a chance to respond, my lawyer stormed in, letting the door ricochet against the wall. “Don’t say another word, Maverick! And you two, what do you think you’re doing? Step away from my client!”

“Relax, we were just chatting with him!” Wilson retorted.

“My client doesn’t have to say anything to you because there’s nothing to say! Where is your evidence, huh? My client has paid his debt to society and for you to have the audacity to accuse him of the murder of his own brother while he is still in mourning sounds like nothing short of harassment to me. So, if you continue to waste our time, I’ll be sure to file a lawsuit against everyone in this precinct to the point where you’ll be wishing you never placed cuffs on him!"

Joel may have been a brittle looking, middle-aged white man, but he showed no weakness, which is exactly what I paid him to do. The two walked out of the room as silent as church mice, leaving the two of us alone.

"What the fuck, Joel?" I asked. I still couldn't believe they had the audacity to think I was behind any of that shit.

"I made some calls on my way down here, just trying to figure out what the hell was going on, and honestly, I wish I had better news."

"What am I up against?"

"The word conspiracy is floating around. They're trying to link your past charges and involvement in the drug business as your motive. If they can make anything stick, they're going to try to use the Kingpin Statute. Minimum thirty years, max is life."

"Kingpin? Come the fuck on, man. I'm done with that shit. How many fuckin' times I gotta say that?"

"You know that, and so do I, but it's not about what we know. It's about what we can prove. The justice system is funny like that. What did they say to you?"

"Nothing much, just somethin' about some cell

phone towers putting me close to the accident."

"Did you say anything to them?"

"No, besides the fact that I was fuckin' his bitch."

Joel sighed. "Goddammit, Maverick. How many times have I told you not to antagonize these investigators? Do you have anything that can put all their questions and suspicions to rest?"

The room fell silent. I knew Suki's cell phone would prove my innocence, but I wasn't ready to give that up yet. I had my own reasons for keeping that close to me.

"No," I answered.

He sighed. "Okay, well until we can make sure all this blows over with no problem, you have to keep your hands clean, and I mean squeaky fuckin' clean. They'll be watching you like a hawk and will try to use anything against you to help them build their case. Don't make it easy for them."

My head bobbed in agreement. "I've been clean. Don't worry, I'm never goin' back to the game or to a cell," I assured him.

"Good. Now, let me go do my job. I'm going to make sure you walk out of here as soon as possible," he assured me.

TWO

River

I *couldn't* believe it.

I'd finally gotten what and who I wanted, and he was taken away from me in the blink of an eye. Flashing lights from the cop cars lined up in the driveway as if they were on a parade route. I watched them put the man I loved in cuffs for the murder of my best friend and his own brother.

"What the hell is going on? Why are you cuffing him? He didn't do anything wrong!" I yelled, searching for some sort of answer as to why they were even there and why any of it was happening in the first place.

Mav's lips moved, but all I could do was stare blankly into his eyes. There was no fear in them, only sadness.

"I'm going to get out, don't worry. Everything is gon' be fine, I fuckin' promise," he said.

Each word sounded muffled as if I was being held underwater against my will. They slammed the car door and proceeded to haul him away as if he was the grand prize at a carnival. My mind was left spinning like a toy top. The dust hadn't fully settled on my *Runaway Bride* shit, and my new happily ever after had been placed on hold because the man I'd chosen was about to be sitting behind bars. If Leander ever got wind of this, he'd say it was my karma. Shit, maybe it was. I never proclaimed to do everything right all of the time, but all I knew was that I loved Mav. I was surely broken and wouldn't be operating at full capacity without him by my side. With no answers, I had to wrap my head around the fact that it would be just me and Noemi until however long. I was grateful she was at a friend's house and wasn't there to witness the commotion and trauma of seeing her uncle put in handcuffs and placed in the back of a cop car for the murder of her parents.

I glanced down at my phone to see Leander's name across the screen. He'd been calling and texting me nonstop, wanting answers I simply couldn't give him. I didn't know how else to tell him my heart was with another man without saying just that. The fact that the tables had turned so drastically was ironic. It wasn't so long ago that I was the one calling every second of the day wanting answers, and now I was the one ignoring calls. I had pulled a *him* on *him*.

Leander: [4:45 p.m.]: *River, baby. Pick up! Let's talk about this. Please.*

Me: [4:47 p.m.]: *There's nothing to talk about. I'm sorry.*

Me: [4:48 p.m.]: *Please stop calling me.*

Leander: [4:49 p.m.]: *Really, River? Because I think we have a lot to talk about. Your bullshit apology for leaving me at the altar for another nigga ain't good enough for me. You embarrassed the fuck out of me in front of my family and yours!*

Leander: [4:50 p.m.]: *Who the fuck is this nigga anyway, huh? Nothin' but fuckin' jailbait when you can be with a man who loves and knows you, River!*

Leander: [4:50 p.m.]: *Does what we have not mean shit to you anymore?*

Leander: [4:53 p.m.]: *Hello? River!*

I sighed, knowing he was barking up the wrong tree. He could talk tough and say whatever he wanted over the phone and over 300 miles away, but he didn't want problems with Mav. Instead of entertaining him any longer, I moved forward with blocking his number. What was done was done, and he had to accept the fact that in our case, love didn't always win.

THE DOORBELL RANG an hour later. I'd had enough surprise pop-ups for one day and was skeptical about answering or not. I dragged my feet over to the door before opening it for a dark-skinned man with long dreads wearing designer eyeglasses.

"River?" he asked.

My brows furrowed. "Who are you?"

"I'm Sosa, Mav's right hand. I've got an update for you."

"Oh my God, please come in," I said, waving him in.

He walked in, and we posted up on opposite sides of the kitchen island. "Are you thirsty? Can I get you something to drink?"

He shook his head. "Nah. Where's Noemi?" he

asked.

"She's at a friend's house. I'm going to go pick her up in another hour or so. I've been wracking my brain trying to come up with something to say to her when she asks where he's at. The three of us were supposed to make homemade pizzas tonight."

"Don't tell her shit. He'll be home before we know it, trust me."

"So, what's going on? You said you had an update for me."

"The lawyer is there with him now. They don't have shit because he ain't do shit. They just tryna flex because of who he is. They took him down once and lookin' for any reason to do it again."

I hadn't fully had time to process Mav's arrest, let alone the reason behind it. I loved him as much as my human heart could, but I would be lying if I said I knew everything about him or his past. All I knew was that Suki wasn't one of his favorite people, and he wasn't the biggest fan of her relationship with his brother either. Was that enough motive for him to kill them? What would he get out of it, and why would he draw that much attention to himself after just getting out?

"Was he with you the night of the accident?" I

asked.

"Nah, he wasn't."

I nodded. "Oh, do you know where he was?"

"No, and I don't need to know because it doesn't matter. He ain't do shit, and that's all I need to know," he said, solidifying whose side he was on.

I drew in a deep breath and blew all the air through my nose. I didn't know Sosa, but if I wanted to get answers about Mav without going to him directly, I knew he'd be my best option. "Did you know he had a brief thing with Suki before Luca came into the picture?" I blurted out, curious to know exactly how much he knew about their past.

He sighed. "Look, I don't know you, and you don't know me. But what I do know is that nigga, Mav, would never do no shit like that, no matter who he fucked, who he loved, who he hated, he's not a dirty nigga like that."

I nodded. "I know."

"Do you? Because if you did, you wouldn't be questioning me about him."

I sighed. "I'm sorry, you're right. I'm not questioning you because I'm suspecting him. I'm questioning you because I just want to know all that I can about him and his past and—"

"Ask him yourself when he comes home because he's coming home," he assured me.

Feeling like a doubting Thomas, my head dropped down as my eyes stared holes into my shoes. He was right. I didn't need to go fishing around for answers. Whatever I wanted to know, I needed to hear it straight from the horse's mouth. "You're right, and I will. He's never lied to me before, and I don't see a reason for him to start now."

Sosa looked me up and down with a look of disapproval written across his face. "He don't need doubters in his camp, I don't give a fuck if he love you or not."

"Look, I get it, you ride for him. I'm not trying to make him out to be a monster, that's not my intention at all," I said, knowing I'd clearly made a terrible first impression with his bestie, and I'm sure he'd waste no time telling Mav that I wasn't down for him in his time of need.

I glanced across the island and saw the cell phone Mav had told me to go through just before he got arrested. If answers were what I wanted, I knew I also needed to take a deeper dive into finding out just who the hell Suki Diamond Malone really was.

"What's that?" he asked, following my eyes to the phone.

I quickly swiped up Suki's phone. "Nothing. It's my old phone. I'm transferring some stuff over. But um, I think I'm about to call and see if Noemi is ready now. Can you uh, just have his lawyer call me when he's ready? Or I can give you my number. I want to be the one to pick him up when it's time."

He eyed me in silence for a few seconds, knowing I was trying to send him on his way. He nodded. "Yeah, I'll let you know."

"Thank you," I said and exchanged numbers before walking him to the door.

I closed and locked the door behind Sosa and raced into the living room with Suki's phone in hand. if I was going to truly be Mav's ride or die, I couldn't allow my own conspiracies cloud my judgment. I pushed the thoughts to the furthest corner of my mind and focused solely on finding out just what my best friend had been up to. If the phone didn't have something important on it, she wouldn't have roped her five-year-old daughter into keeping her secrets.

For the next hour, I listened to voicemails, read text messages, and searched through every nook and cranny of the phone. Going through everything had unearthed so much about Suki that I didn't know, yet I was still sitting with so many unanswered questions. It wasn't hard to tell that she was in trouble with someone, but none of the numbers in her phone were associated with a name, no contact information, or potential photos with faces were stored either. All I knew was that she was making her money behind Luca's back and doing things for it that she didn't need to do given her financial status. What did she need all that extra money for, and what was she planning to do with it? I wanted nothing more than to be able to pick up the phone and call her or pull up to her house and know she'd be there to give me the answers I so desperately craved, but I had to face the fact that was something that would never happen.

Listening to those three voicemails made me sick to my stomach. If she knew she was in trouble, why didn't she tell Luca? She had a man with money, power, and connections that extended across the city if not further—why did she feel like she couldn't tell him what the fuck was really going on when she'd gotten in over her head? I closed my eyes and flashed back to one of my last conversations with Suki about her "new job."

"I'm not sayin' you have to be drippin' in Gucci and gold, but damn, can you try at least something with a name brand?" Suki asked.

"Newsflash, Su! I'm a fuckin' broke ass teacher. I don't have the luxury of having a damn kingpin for a husband to keep me dressed in designer all day, every day."

"Aht-aht! Chill with all that. Yeah, I got it good, but I make my own money now, remember?"

I sucked my teeth. "My bad, I forgot. What is it that you do now, Su?" I asked, knowing damn well her only two talents were being bad and bougie. The girl's middle name was Diamond for Pete's sake. Living the luxury life was all she ever wanted.

"You know what, you're a hater, River Lynn Newman. You really don't believe me?"

"A hater? I don't have a hater bone in my body, and it's not that I don't believe you, but have you forgotten that I've known you all of my life, and I've only ever known you to have two jobs that you lasted for all of two weeks?"

"Okay, but this is different."

"How?"

"It just is, okay? And how did we go from talking about you to talking about me, huh? Stop deflecting, River! I'm tryna show you how to get a man, a paid one at that."

I sighed. I definitely needed to win the lottery in more ways than one. "That would be nice."

"Hell yeah! You know I always got your back, girl.

So it's settled, we goin' out to catch you a baller!"

My eyes flooded with tears as I tried to mentally process the fact that I might never know why she did what she did or why she took three million dollars from someone. I wasn't comfortable with the new image of Suki in my mind. A part of me wanted to go back to the past when I thought I knew her like the back of my own hand. Who was I really friends with for all those years? The older we got, the more I realized we lacked things in common. I wanted a career, she wanted to get paid, by any means necessary, but I never thought her thirst for paper would lead her to an early grave.

As conflicted and emotionally overwhelmed as I was, I had to put all of that to the side and put on a brave face for Noemi.

"Where's Uncle Mav?" Noemi inquired as soon as we got back in the house.

"He's uh, out of town doing stuff for his tattoo shop," I blurted out.

She turned up her nose. "Oh. I thought we were supposed to make pizzas tonight."

"I know, I'm sorry. It was last minute and he told

me to tell you that he'll make it up to you."

"Yeah," she said, casting her eyes down to her shoes.

Thinking quickly on my feet, I asked, "Hey, do you wanna make a fort?"

A bolt of excitement zapped in her eyes. "Can we have a sleepover in it?"

"Yeah, sure! What do we need for our fort?"

"Pillows!"

"Pillows…and what about blankets?" I asked.

"Yeah!"

"And popcorn!" I suggested.

"Yeah! Popcorn!"

"Okay, you go and find some blankets and I'll go pop the popcorn and get some snacks."

"Yay!"

LATER THAT NIGHT, Noemi and I were snuggled up in our makeshift fort in our PJs. "What kind of story do you want to hear tonight?" I asked.

"I want a mommy story."

I sighed. Even though I knew the truth about Suki. It didn't change the fact that Noemi still idolized her. I couldn't taint her image of her mother. "Why don't you tell me one?" I suggested.

"I don't know how to tell a story."

"Of course you do. Who's your favorite storybook character?" I asked.

"Um, Princess Tiana, Moana, and JoJo Siwa."

I chuckled. "Okay, well tell me a story about the time Princess Tiana and Moana meet up with JoJo Siwa and go on an adventure to find a pair of missing magic sneakers."

She giggled. "That's a silly story."

"Get to telling it, missy!"

Noemi talked for forty-five minutes straight before tiring herself out. The girl had the gift of gab.

"Goodnight, Auntie River," she whispered, eyes already closed.

"Goodnight," I told her, lips brushing against her forehead.

THREE

River

I was in the midst of teaching my morning math segment when a wave of nausea hit me like a ton of bricks. I'd been feeling queasy off and on the night before but chalked it up to everything that was going on with Mav and the outpour of Suki's secret life. Luckily, I was able to make it through the majority of the day before spewing my guts out in the bathroom inside the teacher's lounge. After washing my hands, I splashed a few drops of cold water on my face and glanced at my reflection in the mirror. My eyes were puffy since crying seemed to become my new cardio over the past twenty-four hours, and I was sporting a permanent frown. I sighed as I tightened my ponytail and wrapped my bun before pulling my vibrating phone out of my back pocket. The text I was waiting on had finally come in.

Sosa: [12:42 p.m.]: *He'll be processed out in about an hour. You still wanna pick him up?*

Me: [12:43 p.m.]: *Yes, I do. I'm at work, but I'll figure out something. Thank you!!!*

My heart somersaulted in my chest. "Finally!" I squealed.

My eyes tore across my reflection once more. I had to get something together to be able to leave work and put the life back into my face. He didn't need to know how much of a mess I'd been without him. As soon as I exited the bathroom, I headed straight to the main office to try to find someone to cover my classroom for the remainder of the day because I didn't feel well.

IT WAS A DULL AFTERNOON with a gray sky that had been threatening rain all day, so much that I could smell the rain in the air. On my way to pick up Mav, my phone rang again, cutting into my GPS directions. I glanced down at the screen to see Suki's mom calling. As much as I didn't want to be disrespectful, I didn't have the time nor the patience to deal with her mouth or the drama that always flew out of it. I quickly pressed ignore and put my focus back on the road ahead and getting to Mav as quickly as I could. I couldn't wait to lay my eyes on him.

I was sitting outside of the front gate of the prison with my windows rolled down and the cool breeze flowing in, impatiently waiting for Mav to be released. My eyes caught a glimpse of a large man walking him across the gated compound to the front gate, and I quickly popped a stick of gum in my mouth while making sure my lips were glossed and no hairs were out of place. Mav walked out and instantly smiled when he saw me. I got out and ran over to him, crashing my body into his. He wrapped his arms around me, and in those fleeting seconds, I felt more peace than I had in what felt like years.

He quickly lifted my chin and placed his lips on mine. "I've been thinking about doing that since I been in that mothafucka."

I smiled. "I needed that."

"C'mon, let's get the fuck outta here. I don't want to be on the premises of this mothafucka no longer than I need to be."

I nodded, and we got in the car. Once we were on the road to home, Mav reached over and laced his fingers in between mine before kissing the top of my hand.

"Where does Noemi think I am?" he asked.

"I told her you were on a business trip for your shop, so she's fully expecting you to bring her something back. Oh, and she's wanting a re-do of pizza night. She said, *'just because he left doesn't mean he's off the hook!'*" I chuckled.

He grinned. "Thanks for not telling her. I don't want her to see me like this and think this is how shit goes."

"No, I know. I wouldn't dare tell her, especially not until we know more about what's going on. Are you okay?"

"Me? I'm good. This ain't nothin'. The question is, are you okay? You look sick or like you've been crying or something."

"Don't worry about me. I just want to know what the fuck happened in there. My head has been spinning since you were hauled away. I felt so helpless. I couldn't do shit to help you or save you."

"I know, and I'm sorry you had to witness that shit. You did everything you were supposed to do, plus you're here now and that's all that matters."

I nodded before taking my eyes off the road to look at him. "There is something we need to talk about though…"

"You went through the phone?"

"Yeah," I nodded, "I did, and I…I'm still processing. She just left me with so many unanswered questions that I don't know where to start."

"Where's the phone?"

"It's at the house."

"Good, keep it safe. It may be my only leverage if these dick ass cops try to come barking up the wrong tree again."

"I just can't figure out why she stole the money in the first place, or what she did with it. She wouldn't steal that much to spend it all so fast, right?"

"I wouldn't put it past her." He shrugged.

"Maybe its mixed in with her accounts with Luca."

"If he didn't know shit about any of this, how would she explain a deposit that large and the bitch ain't have a job?"

"Watch your mouth!" I reprimanded him.

His voice softened a little. "I'm sorry, but she wouldn't do that shit. He would've noticed immediately. He was too good with numbers."

"Then it's still gotta be around, but where? And why would she take it from…whoever that was on the phone?"

"That's what I don't know, but when we find out, then we'll know who really killed my brother."

"And Suki," I reminded him.

"Yeah."

"But there's more that I need to know that doesn't have anything to do with her."

"What?"

"I need to know what you've done in your past, Mav. All of it. Because when everything happened, I can't lie and say that it didn't cross my mind that you may have had something to do with it. Even as much as I know how deep your love runs for your brother and Noemi, it was still there, gnawing at me like a pesky mosquito that just wouldn't go away. I want to know all of you so that I never have to feel that uncertainty again."

"What if you can't handle it?" he asked, with a savage edge laced in his tone.

"That's my decision to make, but don't you think I deserve to know what I'm getting into if we're going to be together?"

"You're right," he responded with a head nod,

contributing even less to the conversation.

His response struck me as incomplete, so I waited a few seconds for him to finish his thought.

“Well?” I asked. “Tell me the truth, Mav. No more secrets, okay? Because I’ve already got enough fuckin’ secrets to last me a lifetime.”

Mav

She was right. I knew better than most that secrets could isolate you, even from the ones you cared about the most. I’d never come clean to Luca about fuckin’ around with Suki before they became a thing, or the fact that I’d questioned the paternity when I found out she was pregnant. All I ever mentioned to him was that she was out there and just looking to catch a nigga on her line. He’d just happened to be the one to bite.

“Your silence is telling,” she said, breaking my train of thought.

I let out a long breath. She’d already found out who her friend really was, so it was time to give her the truth about the nigga she’d fucked around and fallen in love with. I broke my gaze on the road ahead when River pulled off into a gas station parking lot.

"Fuck you doing?" I asked. "Let's go."

"No."

"If you don't put this mothafucka in drive," I warned.

She killed the engine and folded her arms across her chest. "I'm not going anywhere until you tell me what I want to know. I'm not playin' with you, Mav."

I huffed. I fuckin' hated her stubborn ass sometimes. "Fine. In order for you to know who I am, you need to know how I was raised. Contrary to what you might think, Luca and I weren't brought up in the streets. We lived in a good neighborhood and went to private school with white kids and shit. I wasn't a dumb mothafucka, but I was really only interested in drawing and reading. So naturally, the only two classes I paid any attention in were English and art. Luca, on the other hand, loved math. He was two years younger than me, but the mothafucka was so smart that by the time I was going into high school, so was he."

"Damn, really?"

I nodded. "Yeah. By the time we got to junior year, he'd caught the attention of his advanced calculus teacher, a forty-year-old white mothafucka named Bruce. We called him Batman. He brought him on as an intern at his side-business as an accountant and started teaching him how to run numbers and move money."

"Hold up. A white man put y'all onto the drug game? And Bruce? Like Bruce Wayne?"

I chuckled. "Yeah, like Bruce Wayne. He was just a white mothafucka with money, so he taught us how to manipulate numbers and be smart with money, which is a good thing to know when you are in the game."

"I don't understand—if you weren't hard up for money or didn't really grow up around that lifestyle, what made you want to, you know, go down that path?"

"My father lost his job the summer before our senior year and shit started to go downhill real fuckin' fast. That's when we learned they didn't have a dime in their savings and that meant that if our tuition wasn't paid, we weren't goin' back to graduate. So, he took us on a trip to meet our Uncle Salt, his brother. Up until then, he'd kept us far away from his side of the family, and it wasn't until meeting our uncle that we found out why. Turns out he was heavy in the game, and the Malone family name held weight in the streets and was known all throughout the south. My father had the opportunity to run the family empire alongside his brother, but he chose to go legit. When going legit backfired, he went back to what he knew and asked Uncle Salt for a loan. No lie, we watched that man drop fifty stacks right on the table like it was pennies to him. I'd never seen that much money all at once before in my life."

“Me either.”

“Before my father could get the money, Salt started talking about how he needed more soldiers that he could trust in the streets to move his product. Then that nigga tossed a brick on top of the money. I can still hear his voice clearly in my head. He said, “*If you want it, you gotta move it. Family or not, nothing is fuckin’ free.*”

“So your dad basically offered up both his sons to a life of crime just for money?”

“People have done way worse for way less,” I reminded her, “besides, parenting don’t come with a fuckin’ handbook. You of all people should know that by now.”

She shrugged. “I guess. I just don’t think I could do that to my children.”

“He didn’t do shit to either of us. What he did, he did it for us, so that we could continue to live the life we’d been accustomed to. A life he’d supplied going legit to show us that there was a right way and a wrong way to do shit. It was nothin’ more important to him than us getting an education. He wanted us to be legit too, but we ended up being both.”

“What do you mean?” she asked.

“I spent the rest of the summer learning the game and reading books on stocks, while Luca still worked with his teacher to learn how to move money around and make it all look squeaky fuckin’ clean. With our skills combined, we were able to hide in plain sight. White mothafuckas took one look at us and didn't expect us to be smart, and niggas looked at us and didn't expect us to be about our business. They underestimated us, and we took over everything."

Her creased brow and pouty lips told me she was confused. "So if you were so clean, how'd you get caught up and end up goin' away?"

"Just because we were clean on paper doesn't mean our hands were. The night I got pulled over, I'd met up with Luca to re-up. When we got back to our meet up spot, he took the truck to the warehouse, and I followed behind him in his car to make sure everything went smoothly. We got separated by a red light, and I ended up getting pulled over by some racist mothafuckin' cops just lookin' to come up off a nigga. They pulled me out the fuckin' car, searched the shit illegally, never told me why they pulled me over in the first place and planted a brick on me and hauled my ass off to jail all because of my last name and what they knew my family did."

"Are you fucking serious?"

"Yeah. Neither one of us would've been fuckin' dumb enough to ride around with that much shit on us without it being concealed."

"That's illegal! I mean, what did you do? What can you do now? They should fuckin' be arrested!"

"With that much weight on me, I was facing a federal minimum of ten years, but because of their actions, my lawyer got it down to half that."

"Oh, my God. No, that's not good enough! You need to sue! You need to fight back! Those weren't even your drugs!" she demanded.

"It's not like I could prove it wasn't mine. You already know it was my word against theirs. Turns out, they'd been building a case against my family, trying to pick off corner boys and get them to flip. I guess somebody was finally dumb enough to drop my name and boom—I'm on the radar, you know?"

She was fired up and clearly still unhappy with my situation. She wanted justice to prevail the way she'd seen it done in movies or on TV. Real life just didn't work that way, especially for a Black man in America.

"I just think you should at least have gotten them fired. They should really be in jail!"

Little did she know, they'd been dealt with. The day I was sentenced in the eyes of justice, so were they—in the eyes of the streets. "Trust me, they got what was coming to them. All I had to do was make one phone call."

Her eyes widened. "Are you saying you—you had them…"

"Justice was served," I said, cutting her off.

River sighed just before clasping her hands together in front of her. "I'm not going to say I agree with your methods, but I understand why you did what you did."

"Well, I hope you keep that same energy when I deliver the same fate to the nigga that killed my brother."

"Don't be reckless. I know you want to find out who is responsible, but I also know your brother would not want you being hauled off to jail again. He chose you to raise his daughter. You can't leave her."

"Never that. I don't have any intention of leaving Noemi or you ever again, but I do have to handle this."

"If I can't change your mind about it, can I at least convince you to do it the right way? When you find out who it was, let's take it to the cops. Let's let justice really be served. He should rot in jail for the rest of his life for what he did."

"Why let him make a pitstop on his way to hell? I'd rather just send his ass there myself," I told her.

River silently shook her head. "I just don't get who would try to make enemies with someone with your…status."

"Somebody with a death wish apparently. I'm tellin' you, River, whatever Suki had going on with that nigga, he took it personal. That tells me that he doesn't think shit out and reacts off pure emotion."

"Do you really think she took his money?"

"I don't know why someone would lie about some shit that. Especially not the way that nigga was huffin' and puffin' on those voicemails. He's reckless, leaving paper trails and shit. All that mothafucka is doin' is droppin' breadcrumbs that'll lead me straight to his ass, believe that."

She released a loud sigh. "Who knew having money could be such a terrifying thing?"

"Nah, having *no* money is a terrifying thing. Niggas will lose their mind the second they think they goin' broke. Like I told you, niggas have done way more for way fuckin' less."

"Three million is *a lot* of money."

"And fuckin' with my family means this nigga wrote a check his ass can't cash."

"What exactly are you going to do…when you find him?"

"Just know I'm going to handle it, and it's gotta be quick. I just gotta be extra careful with the case these mothafuckas are tryna build against me, but I'm not gon' stop. I can't."

"Wait, a case? What case? What did your lawyer

say?"

I tucked my bottom lip and then looked directly in her eyes before delivering the truth to her ears. "He said they're trying to build a case against me and hit me with the Kingpin Statute. Mothafuckas want to make something stick so bad. They took the brick they planted on me and linked my last name to my Uncle Salt and the family business. Now, if they can try to prove that I killed my brother to take over the business, then they could put my ass away for life," I confessed.

I never wanted to see pain in her eyes, but I knew telling her the truth would wreck her entire world.

"*L—life*?" she stuttered.

I nodded. "So like I said, I gotta be extra careful, but I'm not gon' stop until I find the mothafucka who took my brother out and put hot lead in his fuckin' skull," I promised her.

WHEN WE GOT HOME, I headed straight for my bedroom. When I walked in, I saw rose petals all over the bed, unlit candles, and a red lingerie set laying across the chaise.

"What is all this?" I asked, turning to see River standing in the doorway.

"Well, I was trying to throw together something special to welcome you home, but after that heavy ass talk we just had, I don't think I'm even in the mood anymore," she admitted while shrugging her shoulders.

"Don't let that shit kill your vibe. They are problems that will still be problems tomorrow. If you wanted to enjoy the night with your nigga, then I'ma give you that. That's the least I can do for you holdin' down the house while I was tucked away for a second."

A smile parted her lips as she walked over to me. "You know I got you."

"Good. Keep fuckin' around and a nigga might put a rock on your finger, and not that little pebble that other nigga had you rockin' either." I chuckled.

A laugh broke past her lips, and we continued to laugh in unison, even though we both knew I was serious.

"Whatever."

"But for real, let me take your mind off things," I said, reaching out to let my hands bracket her waist.

"Okay, but uh…take a shower first because…yeah," she said, pinching the tip of her nose.

"Join me then," I suggested.

"Go ahead and get started without me. I'll be in there in a few."

I turned on the shower and undressed while I let the water heat up. I stepped inside and ran my hands across the dark planked wood aligning the shower walls while letting the water run all over my body. River was right, I had to wash off the stench of those pigs at the precinct and it felt good doing so. Glancing up through the foggy shower door, I saw River walk in wearing the red lingerie set.

"Oh word? That's what you on?" I asked her, while opening the shower door.

She smiled. "I at least wanted you to see me in it."

"You know I love to see you in red, but I'd much rather watch you take it off."

My dick stiffened as I watched her pull her hair down from her bun and drop her bra and panties in front of me. My gaze devoured her beauty, soaking her in like a sponge. A subtle smirk bent my lips. "Goddamn, I missed you."

I pulled her into my arms and let the warm water cascade down our bodies. With my lips pressed against hers, I caressed her figure, lathering her up with soap in the process. Her warm, wet skin felt like butter against mine. My hands roamed freely all over the peaks and valleys of her physique as I reached down to grab a handful of her ass. "I missed this too."

"All of me missed you, Maverick Malone," she said,

ringing her arms around my neck.

I kissed her deeply as my dick pressed against her stomach. I reached down to slide my hands over her curves and in between her thighs. Just as I thought, her pussy was throbbing and anxiously awaiting my touch.

River dropped down to her knees and took me in her mouth. “Mmm, shit. You did miss a nigga, didn’t you?” I groaned as she licked up the tip.

I locked my hands behind my head and watched her draw it in and out of her mouth slowly like the tease she was. Her long, wet hair ran for miles down her back as she reached up to run her hand down my abs. She sucked me slowly, gurgling and gagging as I palmed the back of her head.

“Mmm, shit,” I growled as she started to lick my balls.

No longer wanting to wait, I reached down to pull her up and hold her in my arms again. I lifted her up by her ass cheeks and pressed her back against the shower wall. River’s legs crisscrossed around my waist as she locked her arms around my neck. I pressed my dick against her slit.

“Oooh, yeah.”

“Mmm, this what you been waitin’ for?” I growled.

"Mmhmm," she moaned, biting her lip.

I bit down on my lip as my dick slowly pushed inside her. We both groaned in unison as our bodies merged together as one. Delivering one slow stroke after the other, I pulled River up and down on my length.

"Mmm, this some good ass pussy."

"I missed you so much, Mav," she confessed, moaning between breaths.

"I missed you too," I said against her lips. "Don't worry, I'ma keep strokin' that pussy for you to make up for every second I missed by your side."

I wrapped my hand around her throat and continued to slowly pump inside her. She was screaming and moaning like crazy. I put one of her legs down and lifted the other up over my shoulder, demanding her body to bend to my will.

"Ooooh shit, yessss! Yessss, right there!" she screamed.

I started to pump harder, watching droplets of water drip off her hard nipples.

"Mav, I—I'm cumming," she whimpered.

I pulled her lips onto mine and kissed her deeply before putting her leg back down. "Daddy wants you to cream all over this dick again. You gon' cum all over this dick?" I asked.

She nodded repeatedly as her eyes rolled back in her head.

"Now turn around," I said, spinning her body around. I was going to make sure she knew that more than just my dick missed her.

I started planting a trail of kisses up the back of her legs, to her thighs, and the arch in her back before sliding my tongue between her pussy lips from behind. My tongue lapped up the water pouring down her body like a waterfall as she squirmed underneath my grasp.

"Dammmmnnnn, that feels soooo fuckin' gooood. I'm gonna cuummmmm," she hummed, sinking her teeth into her bottom lip.

I swayed my mouth and tongue from side to side, making sure my name was written all over her kitten while sliding my fingers deep inside her warmth.

"Mmm, shit, I'm so wet. Fuckin' give it to me, baby."

"You need the D again?" I asked, coming up for air.

"Mmhm, I need it," she panted.

I pressed her body up against the shower door,

hooked my arm around her waist, and buried every inch of my dick deep inside her. She looked back at me, moaning against my lips. Gathering a handful of her wet hair in my hand, I yanked her head back while flicking her swollen clit with my thumb.

"Oh shit! Oh fuck!"

"I bet that other nigga never fucked you like this," I affirmed.

"Never, baby!"

"You're mine, forever," I growled in her ear.

"I'm yours, baby. All yours," she purred.

River leaned her head back as she arched her back deeper, taking all of my dick like a straight G. I kissed her forehead and then snaked out my tongue to lick her lips as she threw it back against me. "Yeah, that's right, fuck that dick!" I commanded.

Her hands were firmly planted against the shower wall for support as I relished in the sound of my wet skin smacking against hers.

Changing positions, I sat down on the built-in shower seat and pulled her on top of me. With her hair tossed over her face, she leaned in close and slowly started to slide up and down my pole.

"Mmm shit, I love this pussy," I said, before smacking her ass.

She squealed out as she bounced up and down. Her ass jiggled in my hand as I grabbed and smacked it, sending water splashing.

"Oooh shit, yeah! Yeah!"

"Yeaaahh, make that fuckin' pussy cum!" I commanded, as my teeth lightly gnawed at her hard nipples.

"Mmm, fuck, baby!"

"Shiiiiiiiitttttt," I groaned, feeling myself about to nut.

I thrusted hard inside of her until I came. My body shook as I dug my nails into her small waist. Breathing heavily, she turned around to face me. "Round two in the bedroom?" she asked.

I smiled. "Let's go."

River

I woke up to a text from Suki's mom, telling me she was in the city and asking to meet me downtown in an hour.

Mrs. Lawrence [10:37 a.m.]: *River, I'm in town. I hope you can meet me today around noon. I have something important to discuss regarding Suki. If you love her like you say you do, you'll meet me.*

I sighed. I didn't appreciate her trying to guilt trip me since I'd been ducking and dodging her calls, but I went ahead and agreed to show up anyway.

Me [10:40 a.m.]: *Send the address, and I'll be there.*

I stretched and slowly made my way out of the entrapment of Mav's warm grasp. We'd been up for hours, eaten breakfast with Noemi, and crawled back in the bed to have a lazy day together. As much as I didn't want our private little oasis to end, I knew I couldn't ignore Suki's mom any longer.

"Where you going?" he asked.

"Downtown…Suki's mom is in town, and she wants to meet with me."

"I thought I told her ass she needed to stop going through you if she wanted to see Noemi."

"This isn't about Noemi. It's about Suki."

"What about her?"

"That's what I'm going to go find out. She was really vague, just saying she had some important information about Suki that she wanted to talk to me about."

"Mmm," he grunted. "Have fun."

I rolled my eyes before closing the bathroom door behind me. "Gee, thanks."

THE SMELL OF freshly brewed coffee and warm caramel wafted past my nose as I stepped inside the coffeehouse. What once was a welcomed aroma to me, quickly turned my stomach sour for some reason. Since I wasn't much of a coffee drinker, I'd never been there before and didn't know what to get. I glanced down at my phone to read a text from Mrs. Lawrence and then saw her waving at me through the giant glass window. After deciding on what to get and paying for it, I walked outside and found her seated at a secluded bistro table facing the street.

"I'm glad you could join me," she said, standing to give me a hug.

"How have you been?" I asked.

"Some days are better than others, as I'm sure you know. It's been months, but I don't think the pain of losing a child will ever completely go away. How's Noemi doing?"

I took a sip of my warm, milky latte. "She's good."

"Tell her I will Facetime her tomorrow."

I found myself staring at the frothing machine through the giant glass window as she continued on with her small talk. All I wanted to do was get back to Mav and Noemi as quickly as I could to continue or lazy day together as three peas in a pod. "Okay, I will. Now, can you tell me whatever important information you had about Suki?"

"What's the rush, River? Do you have somewhere else to be?" she quizzed.

My head shook in protest. "No, I'm just not feeling the best," I admitted, glancing down at my breakfast muffin with only one bite mark in it.

Cars whizzed down the busy city street as pedestrians walked past, lost in their own little conversations.

"Your face does look a little flushed," she commented.

It took everything in me not to roll my eyes. "So, anyway…"

"I had an autopsy performed on Suki's body," she blurted out.

"What? Why an autopsy? Did you not think she died from the accident?"

"At first I didn't question it, then my lawyer advised me that it might be good to have if things really took a turn for the worst with the whole custody thing with that heathen of a man that's raising her. I still don't know how they could entrust a man like that to protect the hair on her precious little head. I would've been a much better choice," she ranted.

"How can you be so sure?"

"Excuse me?"

"All I'm saying is that Suki and Luca both signed those papers on their will. They wanted Mav to raise their daughter in the event that anything happened to them."

"He's a violent man. Have you seen his rap sheet? Aggravated assault, drug trafficking, I mean this list goes on, River. And not to mention, Noemi's safety! I couldn't live with myself if anything happened to her or you!"

That was it. I couldn't hold it in anymore and unleashed the biggest eye roll I could muster up. "Noemi is fine. Everybody is fine and will stay fine, okay? She absolutely adores Mav, and they have a good relationship together. When are you going to stop trying to get in the way of that?"

She let out an irritated huff. I was never raised to disrespect my elders, but she always harped on how much of a demon Mav was, and she didn't know the first thing about him. If she did, maybe she'd actually shut up for once and eat her own words.

"You sure are making it clear where you stand, River."

"Yeah, I am."

"But do you know where he was that night? Or did he just put it on you so good you didn't even bother to ask?"

The bitter tone in her voice was enough to make me hit the roof. My jaw tightened as I tried to refrain from laying her ass out and leaving. I had to keep reminding myself she was my best friend's mother, and a second mother to me growing up as well.

"Listen," I sighed, "I don't have to ask him where he was because he didn't do it…he wouldn't."

"How can *you* be so sure?" she asked, posing my own question back to me. "I mean, there's no harm in asking him is there? Just to be sure and put all doubts to rest. Then, you'll know the man you love isn't a murderer…*or will you*?"

I frowned. "With all due respect, Mrs. Lawrence, you need to stop. I'm not going to sit here and let you keep talking shit just because you can. I told you everybody is fine, okay? If I felt like anything was wrong, then you know this would be a completely different conversation, but I don't. So just drop it, okay?"

The two of us shared a silent death stare match before she blustered out a deep breath. "Anyway, I want to share the results of the report with you."

"Why would I need to see the results?" I asked.

She handed me the report. "Take a look for yourself."

My eyes darted from left to right as I scanned the report. It was clear that the trauma her body received wasn't all from the impact of the crash, but actually happened after. Air stalled in my lungs as I kept reading—only to find out that Suki had also been seven weeks and four days pregnant.

"Sh—she was pregnant?" I whispered in shock.

"My baby died while carrying another life inside of her, River," she cried.

I clasped my hand over my mouth. "Oh, my God. I wonder if she knew."

"I don't know," she sighed, "I thought the report would bring closure…but I swear to God, I wish I'd never found out."

A sudden upsurge of nausea rolled through my body as my brain started hammering against my skull. "Whoa."

"Are you okay?"

"Y—yeah, I just got a little dizzy all of a sudden."

"I know it's a lot to take in."

"Will you excuse me for a minute?" I asked. I quickly darted up from the table and back inside the coffeeshop to the restroom. After tossing up the breakfast muffin and latte, I swished around some sink water in my mouth and quickly spit it back out in the sink. If there was one thing I hated, it was throwing up. I hated not having full control over my body and its functions.

When I walked back out to the table, Suki's mother was still seated.

"How are you feeling?" she asked while reaching out to touch my hand.

I nodded. "I'm okay. I think I should be getting home though."

"Maybe you should pick up a pregnancy test on the way…"

My forehead creased. "Excuse me? Why would I need a pregnancy test?"

She quickly shrugged her shoulders. "The flushed face, the picky eating, nausea…I've been pregnant before, River, and the symptoms are always the same."

"Can you just drop it? I don't need to take a test because I'm not pregnant," I confirmed.

"Whatever you say. But before you go, I also asked you here to give you something else," she said, digging inside her Louis Vuitton handbag.

"What is it?"

"Here," she said, handing me a gold heart locket on a chain.

"What's this?"

"It's for you. Suki told me if anything happened to her, to give it to you..." she said, wiping fresh tears from her eyes.

I was immediately overcome with emotion all over again and could feel tears welling up in the back of my eyes. "Why would she think something was going to happen to her?"

I watched her look over her shoulders and lean in closer to me. "I think she was planning to leave Luca and when she confronted him about it, maybe he got mad. Maybe he tried to flex his manhood and show her who was really in charge. Maybe he got his brother to help. I don't know! All I know is my daughter is dead and it wasn't due to a car accident!"

My brows creased in confusion. "What? Why would she leave him? She loved Luca and her life with him."

"Listen to me, River," she said, leaning across the table and grabbing my shoulders, "a week before she died, she came to me and gave me that necklace. There was this fear in her eyes—I'd never seen it before. A mother knows when there's something wrong with her child, no matter how old they are."

"What else did she say to you? Did she explicitly say she was leaving Luca? Did she say anything that would even make you think that?"

"No, but I know she was planning something."

She was right about that. I knew better than to tell her about the money and what her daughter was really into, but it was interesting to hear that she'd gone to her mother just before things went down. I was even more intrigued to hear that she'd somehow roped me into it with the necklace.

"Do you know how Luca made his money, Mrs. Lawrence?"

She quickly shook her head. "I don't ask questions I don't want to know the answers to."

I nodded. "Okay, well, did she ever mention having a job to you?"

"Her job was being a mother, River. You know that."

Her answers made it clear that Suki had closed her off just like she'd done me. I quickly stood to my feet while bobbing my head up and down. "Yeah, you're right. Well, thank you…for the necklace and stuff…"

"River, if you knew something you'd tell me, right?"

I nodded slowly. "Of course, but I'm sorry, Mrs. Lawrence, I don't know any more than you do."

"Okay, well take care of yourself."

I reached out to hug her again. "Yeah, you too."

THE MOMENT I got back inside my car, I couldn't wait to call Mav and tell him everything I'd found out. Before I could click his name, I found myself doubled over and puking outside my car door onto the pavement.

"What the fuck!" I groaned, while dabbing my lips with an old Chick-Fil-A napkin from my glove compartment.

I quickly went to my calendar and noticed that I had my last period a few weeks before the wedding. "Fuck," I mumbled before resting my head against the headrest and closed my eyes.

Just put the suspicions to rest, River. Get a test and

be done with it, I thought to myself.

There was no way I was going to take the test at home with Mav there, so I stopped at the first convenience store I saw, bought a test, and quickly darted to the back of the store to find the restroom. I paced back and forth for three minutes, waiting for the test to confirm what I already knew—that I wasn't fucking pregnant. When my timer went off, I dashed back over to the sink and froze. There on the edge of the sink was a positive pregnancy test staring back at me.

"Oh shit…"

Mav

I was down at my shop restocking materials when my phone rang. I saw my Uncle Salt's name pop up on my phone and headed back into my office before pressing accept and putting the phone to my ear.

"Uncle, what's up?" I answered.

"How are you, nephew?"

"Maintaining, you?"

"Every day I wake up above ground is a great day, even the shitty ones," he said, dropping wisdom early into the conversation.

"Facts."

"I was just calling to check in on you. We haven't

spoken in a while."

"I've got a lot of shit on my plate," I stated.

"And would one of those things involve your brother?"

"Yes," I admitted, "I'm going to find out who took him from us and when I do, we both know what I'm going to do. That ain't no question."

"I understand your rage, believe me I do. I've lost many close to me over the years, but I want you to be smart about this. I know you want your revenge, and you will have that. I promise you that, on my brother's life. May God rest his soul. You're one of the smartest mothafuckas I know, nephew. Don't lose that on your quest for revenge."

"I don't know if I'll show restraint if given the opportunity, Unc. I just don't. And that's just me keepin' it one-hunnit with you. I feel like I'm on fuckin' borrowed time. I got the feds breathin' down my neck, I got Noemi to raise, my girl, my shop, and still trying to avenge Luca. I gotta do this."

We both knew there was no changing my mind about it, so instead of pressing the issue any longer, he let out a long sigh. "I'll just say this, sometimes you don't always need to be the one behind the trigger to get your desired outcome. Think about that."

We continued to talk about the business and my plans to go legit. As much as he didn't like the idea of me fully stepping away from the family business, he understood the shift in my priorities.

A FEW DAYS LATER, I was finally able to link up with Sosa to talk about business and give him an update on everything goin on with the case they were trying to build against me.

"Kingpin Statute? What the fuck?" he asked.

I nodded as I hit my blunt. "Yeah, so I gotta keep my shit clean, but that doesn't mean that I'm giving up on this Luca shit."

"Speaking of Luca, remember when I told you about that money shit? Well, I figured out what's been going on."

"I'm listening."

"There was money being wired into a separate account for the past eight months. I traced it back to an LLC. I looked into it, and it's under a parent company named Charter Investment Group. They own a lot of commercial real estate properties across the city like bars, restaurants, a couple of strip malls, and a club downtown called Club Mirage."

"How frequently was it coming in?" I asked him.

"Bi-weekly."

"Same amounts?"

"Yup, fifty thousand every time, but it stopped."

"When?"

"There was only one payment sent after Luca's death, nothing after that."

I slammed my glass down on the table. "Fuck! Why didn't I know about this sooner?"

"Your brother had a consecutive process on how he moved his money around, so this account wasn't something that I would've normally noticed. He never mentioned it to me before, so whatever this was, he had a separate arrangement going on outside of the way we normally handled business."

"What club did you say was under that parent company?"

"Uh, Club Mirage," he replied.

"Yo, hold up," I said, thinking back to my conversation with Lauren.

"Wait…oh shit. That was your brother? I remember hearing something about that. Was it a car crash or something?"

"What exactly did you hear?" I pressed.

She shook her head. "No, nothing. I'm sorry, I shouldn't have said anything. I know it's a tough subject for you, and I don't want to make anything worse."

"What did you hear?" I asked again.

"I heard exactly what you said. I was out at Club Mirage with a couple of my girlfriends a few weeks ago, no names or anything, just that a someone died, and it didn't seem like so much of an accident, if you know what I mean."

"And did you believe it?"

She shrugged. "It doesn't matter what I believe. I wasn't there, so I'll never know. No one will."

"Had you known it was me they were talking about before we started working together, would you have done business with me?"

"To be honest, if the money is right, I'll damn near work with anyone," she admitted.

Not only was Club Mirage the place where Lauren had heard the rumor linking me to my brother's death, but it was also likely to be one of the places where Luca had our product running through since it was linked to the same company that was wiring the money into the account. I knew the moment I showed my face back out in Atlanta's nightlife, every nigga in the city would be on me, but I had to go to that club and see if I could get some much-needed answers.

"What?" Sosa asked, jolting me back to the present.

"I think I just found our loose fuckin' end."

"So, what you wanna do?"

"We gon' do what we do best. Step out and make the whole fuckin' city go wild. It'll draw out something, I'm sure of it."

River

Between the breast tenderness, tiredness, missed period, and nausea out of the ass, I could no longer deny the fact that I was pregnant. Not only was I carrying my ex-fiancé's baby, but I had no idea how I was going to tell Mav or Leander, for that matter. Against my wishes, he still hadn't completely given up calling. I kept going back and forth on if I should give him the closure he'd been begging for, but how could there be closure with an unexpected pregnancy? Starting a family with Leander was the only thing I'd ever dreamed about at one time or another, but having it come to fruition when we were no longer together was something I hadn't fathomed.

Life was heavy as fuck, and I was seconds away from crumbling under the pressure. I had way too many balls in the air—Suki's secrets, the looming thought that Mav could be taken away for life for something we knew he didn't do, raising Noemi and now a new baby. We were already technically a "blended" family, but there was no way bringing a new baby and his or her father into the fold would be something Mav or Leander would easily agree to. They both wanted me to themselves, and I knew spreading myself between Atlanta and Chicago would be nearly impossible. As much as I needed a shoulder to lean on, I didn't have a single soul to turn to. Would Mav even understand? After all, it wasn't like Leander was some random one-night stand, I was going to become his lawfully wedded wife just seconds before Mav showed up. But at the same time, if I chose not to move forward with the pregnancy, did Leander even deserve to know?

Tears filled my eyes as I pulled up in the parking lot at my gynecologist's office. Maybe after finding out more about the pregnancy, I'd be able to gain some clarity on what I was going to do. I straightened my posture when I heard a knock on the exam room door. "Come in."

"Hi, River. How are you feeling today?" Dr. Crawford asked, while swiping her salt and pepper hair behind her ears.

"I've been better…do you have the results?"

"Yes, I do, and yes, you are pregnant."

I sighed. Even though I'd already knew the truth, there was a part of me that hoped it had all been a fluke. "So, what is my next step?" I asked.

"Well, your next step is to get an ultrasound scheduled so we can check in to make sure everything is going well with the pregnancy so far."

I paused. "And what if I don't want to, um…you know," I stammered, unable to even say the word terminate or abortion.

Dr. Crawford reached out and rested her hand on my shoulder. "Some may consider an abortion the *easy way* out, but it's *never* an easy decision. At the end of the day, no one can make the decision but you. It's your body, River. You call the shots."

"When would I need to let you know my decision?"

"Well, as soon as possible. I know this isn't

something that should be taken lightly, but I wouldn't be doing my job if I didn't offer you other options like adoption, or—"

I shook my head. "No, it's okay. You've done more than enough, Dr. Crawford. Thank you."

"Well, at least take a couple of these pamphlets with you to read up on different options," she said, handing me three different ones. "There are hotlines on there where you can talk to someone if you don't feel comfortable talking to people in your inner circle about this."

She didn't know how wrong she was. There was no one I could talk to. In fact, the only person I could talk to about it that would understand was Suki, and she was dead. I folded them up and shoved them inside my purse, knowing I'd toss them in the first trashcan I could find as soon as I left her office. "Thank you."

I walked out of the office with my heart still as heavy as it was before I'd gone in. There wasn't a pamphlet on this earth that could make my decision for me. The best option I had was to hide my symptoms as best as I could until I figured out my next move.

WHEN I GOT HOME, I heard Mav's baritone voice in the distance followed by giggles from my favorite little girl. I walked past the stainless steel double ovens and brushed my hand against the marble countertop. "And just what do we have going on here?" I asked, staring at Noemi and Mav standing at the cooktop.

"You wanna eat at our restaurant, Auntie River?"

"Are you a chef?" I asked, tossing my bag on the kitchen island.

"Yeah!"

"Tell me about your restaurant. What's on the menu?"

"It's a surprise! Sit down! We will fix you a plate and bring it to you!"

"Oh, are you my waitress?"

"No, I'm the chef! He's the waiter," she corrected me.

I couldn't help but laugh. "My bad, Chef Noemi."

Mav walked over to me and placed a plate with a cover on top in front of me. "Your dinner is served."

I anxiously removed the top off my plate and a quick laugh broke from my lips as I looked down at the scoops of Kraft Mac and Cheese and two boiled hotdogs on my plate. "Um…is this it?"

"Yup! Taste it!" Noemi nudged me.

"It was our first time making mac and cheese without you," Mav admitted, "so go easy on us."

As nauseating as the mixed smells were, I forced a smile before slicing up my hot dog and forcing it down with a spoonful of mac and cheese. "Wow, it's perfection," I said, kissing my fingertips. "Kudos to the chef and her very handsome waiter!"

I quickly put the top back over my plate and stepped away from it. As thoughtful as their gesture was, I couldn't bear to force down another spoonful of anything. It was moments like that, that made me think of how great it would be for Mav, Noemi, a new baby, and myself the four of us and our misadventures through life with kids. But my life was no fairy tale and we were not in a movie. I knew better than to underestimate Maverick Malone, but I was almost 100 percent certain that he would not be comfortable raising another man's child that wasn't his own flesh and blood.

Mav

I pulled up to Club Mirage with Sosa on my left and my gun tucked away on my right. I needed to know how all the pieces connected, and I was sure something or someone in that club would tell me. We walked straight past a line of people outside waiting to be let in. The smell of liquor, loud, and hot wings met us at the door. Neon strobe lights pulsed to the beat as the DJ shouted out all the birthday girls and bad bitches in attendance. There were dancers on platforms, dancing to every song the DJ played, working the crowd. While half-naked waitresses serviced the VIP area and bar. They were all exotic looking like they'd each been plucked from each continent around the globe. Sosa and I moved through the large space and surveyed from the outskirts.

"Peep your three o'clock," he mumbled.

I looked and saw a light-skinned nigga with a bald-head and full beard making his way over to us, so we headed in the direction of to the bar. The bartender placed my drink on a square napkin and slid it towards me. I tossed it back; the straight shot of tequila felt like a bee sting to the chest.

"Who runs this mothafucka?" I asked Sosa over the loud music.

"I think I can answer that one for you, Mr. Malone, or should I say the man of the hour? Welcome to my club, I'm Sebastian Keyes," a voice echoed behind me.

I turned to see the mothafucka standing all but two feet away from me draped in Givenchy from head to toe. He looked and smelled like a hood nigga who had just hit a lick and wasn't ashamed about it. With a quarter-million-dollar chain hanging around his neck, he was shining so much, everyone in Atlanta was going to think he was the plug. We both knew that wasn't the case.

"How the fuck you know me?"

"When they told me two mothafuckas skipped past my line without so much as a whisper, I asked around about you."

"Oh yeah? And what they say?"

"They say the gates of hell opened up and spit you

out. Is that true?"

I slid my glass away from me. "Most people don't like to find out."

He chuckled. "Hey, we're all friends here. I'd very much like to talk business with you. Please, let's go up to my VIP area to talk privately."

I shook my head. "I don't do business with strangers, and I'm not your fuckin' friend," I said, sizing him up.

"Maybe I phrased that wrong. What I meant to say was unfinished business."

I shrugged him off. "I don't have any business with you, let alone unfinished."

"Apologies, I assumed that the deal your brother and I had would continue under whatever new leadership is coming. Unless…"

I quickly raised my hand to silence him. "What business did you have with my brother?"

"Please, can we go somewhere quieter first?"

"Lead the way."

Sosa and I got up and he stopped. "Just you and I."

"He stays with me," I informed him.

Nodding, he led us through the crowd and into a back room. As soon as he closed the door, I started up.

"So, what unfinished business did you have with my brother?"

"As I was saying, your brother and I had the same interests, a symbiotic relationship of sorts. Simply put, he had the supply, and I had the demand, so I approached him with a money opportunity."

"What kind of money opportunity?" I quizzed.

"The type that involves running your product through my club and cleaning the money in the process."

"Yeah, about that…you got product, but we ain't got no payment," Sosa chimed in.

"And now we got a fuckin' problem," I told him. I reached around for my gun, and Sosa grabbed my arm. I looked back at him and nodded, knowing a premature decision could make the entire house of cards collapse.

He slowly raised his hands in surrender. "Listen, I'm not trying to be enemies. I very much would like to be your friend."

"When you have the money you owe, then I'll know

what type of man you are."

"That's fair. I'll be in touch."

Sosa and I walked out, and I followed the red exit sign staring me in the face. I didn't respect a nigga who wanted to talk new business when he still owed an old debt. Whatever he had going on with Luca was his business, but he didn't know me.

"If that nigga has the demand he says he does and is able to move the weight, I understand why Luca made the deal. I just don't understand why the fuck he didn't tell me," Sosa said after we were back inside the car.

I shrugged and shook my head at the same time. "I know."

"You think he's trying to make his way into the fold?"

"I think he's a nigga with too much money and too much time on his hands who got in over his head and likes pretending to be a boss."

"What are you going to do? You gon' do business with him?"

"Nothing until I know more about this Sebastian nigga, so I need you to look into him. I wanna know where his mama stay, what he ate for breakfast two days ago, and most importantly, his next fuckin' move. Until then, not a word to anybody about any of this."

The car fell silent as Sosa nodded, but I knew he knew what to do. I needed to know how plugged in Sebastian Keyes was, how deep he was into the game, and what type of man I was dealing with.

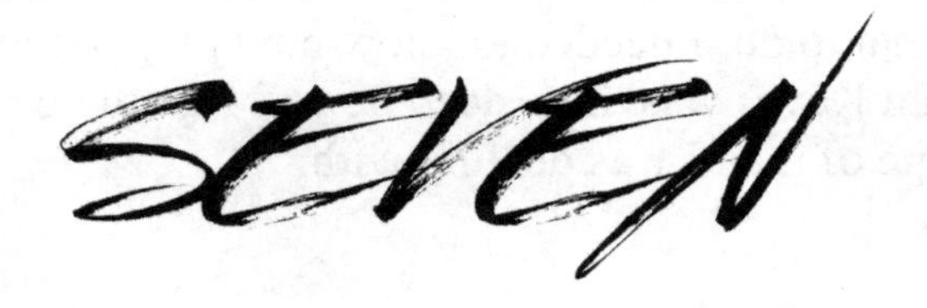

Sebastian Keyes

I may not have been born and bred in Fulton County, but all of Atlanta's nightlife knew the name Sebastian Keyes, and now Maverick Malone was no different. I'd been wanting to run into him for some time but kept my distance. When I got word he was parting the sea of people in my club as if he was Moses, I had to see what all the fuss was about. Needless to say, I was completely unimpressed after our first encounter. He was just another nigga to me. He wasn't God. He wasn't the king of the city or any of the shit I'd expected him to be. He was simply a pawn in my game that I needed to get off the board. A nigga could easily be bought or broken; I just had to figure out which one he'd succumb to first.

After our initial conversation and what I already had heard about him in the streets, it was easy for me to see that he had a lot on his plate. Having a lot on his plate meant he was distracted, which was good news for me. The more distractions that came his way, the easier it would be for me to get what I wanted. Any wise men knew that revenge was a dish best served cold and little did he know that our unfinished business was more than just an unpaid debt. The two of us had more in common than he even knew, and I had a heart of pure ice to prove it. Suki had wronged me in the worst way, and I was going to pick off everybody she loved or was close to if I had to in order to get *my* money back.

When I first set my sights on the Malone family, I made sure I did my research on Luca and his entire family and Lamont "Salt" Malone. The first thing I learned was that the Malone name was well-regarded throughout the streets. The second was that Maverick was locked up on drug trafficking charges. I knew if I wanted to start making a name for myself in the game, they were the *winning team* and the ones I needed to get in good with. Being that Maverick was already in jail, I planned to target his brother, Luca, and then I met *her*. Suki's beauty was almost too much to handle, and there was nothing more dangerous than a sexy ass woman who knew she was sexy.

I quickly became obsessed with everything about her. I'd never met another woman like her in my life. Mama always said I'd know the one when I met her, and she was it. I figured she was the weaker target and if I could drive a big enough wedge between them, she'd choose me in the end. All I had to do was convince her that I was the better man. She enjoyed the chase at first, letting me spend money on her and shower her with gifts. Not once did she make it *easy* for me, but I loved the thrill of her almost as much as I loved her. I thought what we had was real, but she never really gave a fuck about me.

When I found out she was fuckin' around with other niggas, I lost it. Lucky for me, I had friends in high places, and I was able to put a tracker on her car and started following her around the city. It killed me to watch her give away her body to a variety of men. The body that I *worshipped* and would do anything for. I never understood how a woman who already had access to everything, could ever want could resort to doing such degrading things for money she already had.

When we went to meet up at our favorite hotel, I confronted her about her actions in the parking garage before stepping onto the elevator. What started as me threatening to tell Luca everything she was doing behind his back, turned into apologies, tears, and her topping me off before we got to our floor. We stepped off the elevator and went to our suite. After that, all I remember is the two of us having a couple drinks and talking before we ended up fuckin'. We *always* ended up fuckin'.

When I woke up, I was in the hospital and on the brink of death. Turns out, she'd tried to poison me by putting Visine in my drink. When I was out cold, she accessed my bank account information and robbed me blind. All my money was gone and so was she. That's when I knew she was the one behind it. She used my feelings for her against me and almost took my life. I pulled some strings and was able to get the video footage from the elevator and threatened that if she didn't give me back everything she'd stole, I'd blow her entire fuckin' life up. In the end, I made good on my threats and killed the woman I was in love with, with my own two hands.

Although she was dead and gone, she was still making life hard for me. It was because of her that I didn't have the money to pay for the last shipment Luca had delivered to me. Every last red cent I had was in the account that Suki hacked or already had tied up in other things. Although I had money coming in from the club, I owed a lot of people for a lot of different things, so I never really saw too much of that money. Truthfully, I was months away from eviction and possibly days away from having to sell my designer clothes for cash. I was at the point where I had to fake it 'til I made it. I just had to hold out long enough to get back on top.

My legacy would be created by taking down the Malone family. People would talk about me for years to come; how I was the one who did the impossible. I was going to strip Maverick Malone of his pride and break him. Jail wasn't good enough for him. I wanted to hit his ass in a thousand different spots all at once and bring him to his knees. In a perfect world, he would go down for my crimes, but I would have been just as happy to put two bullets in his brain. In the meantime, I would play his little game until it no longer suited me, and then I'd attack. I was going to kill Maverick Malone, or I was going to die trying.

THE NEXT MORNING, I woke up to the smell of bacon sizzling in hot grease and the sound of glassware clicking in the kitchen. My stomach slightly grumbled as I sluggishly rolled over and got up to go brush my teeth. As I turned the corner to the kitchen, my eyes landed on Lauren cooking in nothing but a t-shirt and thong. She already had two plates on the countertop with fluffy scrambled eggs and a short stack of pancakes drenched in warm butter and maple syrup. My tongue darted out of my mouth as I licked my lips before shooting her a slow smile that gradually turned into a wide one.

"Damn, was the dick so good that I deserved a home cooked breakfast?" I asked, before smacking her ass.

She cheesed. "I guess so."

"You got it smellin' good as hell in this mothafucka. I don't think I've ever even cooked in my own kitchen."

"Trust me, it wasn't hard to tell. Luckily, you actually had food in the fridge."

I nodded before ducking my head into the refrigerator and pouring myself a glass of orange juice. Lauren was my real estate agent that I used to acquire a lot of my properties around the city. Our relationship had only turned physical a few months prior, and it was safe to say that since she was practically cookin' in my kitchen butt-ass naked, I had her wrapped around my finger.

I pulled my plate in front of me and tore off a bite of bacon with my teeth. "So listen, I'm interested in a client of yours. I ran into him at my club."

"Who?"

"Maverick Malone," I said, before cutting into my stack of pancakes.

Her eyes widened for a split second and then went back to normal. "What about him?"

"I just want to know what kind of guy he is, that's all."

"A paid one."

"Oh yeah?" I asked, sounding surprised.

"Yeah, paid for his shop in straight cash."

"Liquid funds, huh? Keep talking."

She shook her head. "I feel like I've already said enough. I don't want you thinkin' I go around airing my clients' dirty laundry. I'm not a gossip."

"How much will it take for you to become one?" I

inquired.

She smirked. "Depends on who's asking."

I returned a warm smile to her before walking over and pulled her into my arms. "Name your price," I said before pulling her lips onto mine.

Lauren looked down at the imprint of my dick through my basketball shorts and then flashed her eyes back up at me. "I think I might let you pay me in D just this once."

"You can have every inch of this wood whenever you want, but first, what can you tell me?"

She shrugged. "I don't know much for real. He hasn't been making waves like that ever since he got out of jail and his brother died."

Taking Maverick down meant having the right connections, both legal and illegal. I had to make it my business to know what she knew. I had only mentioned his name once, and she was already emitting what she knew about him. That showed me that if I kept throwing dick and money her way, she would continue to be my eyes and ears. Little did she know that I would have to handle her after I had no more use for her. No loose ends, period. Every move I made had to be calculated. I was going to play her ass like an easy game of checkers until I had total control of the board.

River

I was held up in my car in the school parking lot with a throbbing headache and staring at my vibrating phone with Leander's name blaring across the screen. I'd made the mistake of unblocking him, and as soon as I did, the influx of missed calls, deleted voicemails, and unread text messages returned. If he was anything, he was persistent when he wanted to be. I let out a loud, aggravated sigh, knowing it was time I finally gave in and answered one of Leander's daily calls.

"Hello?" I answered while putting the phone up to my ear.

"River? H—hello?"

"Yeah, Leander. I'm here."

"What the fuck! Finally! I've been calling you for weeks now!"

"And you know exactly why I haven't been answering. I told you everything I had to tell you at the church that day. I'm sorry, I truly am, but I don't know what more you expect from me. My feelings haven't changed."

"What about everything we were trying to build together? We were supposed to get married and start a family, and—"

"Leander, please stop," I said, cutting him off.

I'd been agonizing over if telling him about the baby was the right thing to do or not. Every time I got up the nerve to say it, I chickened out. I suspected that this time would be no different. My heart thumped loudly in my chest. It was now or never. "But listen, the only reason I answered was because I think there is something you should know, I just don't exactly know how to tell you…"

"When have you ever had a problem speaking your mind? You forget I know you, River? Like, really know you?"

I huffed. "Leander, I—"

Before the word *pregnant* broke past my lips, my phone beeped. Mav was calling, and I couldn't have been more relieved.

"You what, River? Finish your sentence," Leander said.

"I'm sorry. I—I have to go," I said and clicked over to answer Mav. I'd chickened out yet again, but I didn't care. I just couldn't bring myself to tell Leander the truth, and I didn't know when I would. "H—hello?" I answered.

"What time do you get off again?" Mav questioned.

"1:45, why?"

"I'm about to pull up on you."

"What? Right now? For what?"

"I need to see you. Shoot me the address, and I'll be on my way."

FIFTEEN MINUTES LATER, he pulled into the vacant parking spot beside me. We both got out at the same time.

"Hey," I said, reaching out to hug him.

"You aight?" he asked.

"Y—yeah, I'm just tired, and I've got a bit of a headache," I admitted. "What did you want to talk to me about that couldn't wait until I got home?"

"Ow! Oh shit, ow!" I squealed, gripping the side of my stomach in pain.

"What's wrong?"

"I don't know, I—shit, ow! I'm having these sharp

pains in my stomach."

"You want me to take you home so you can go lay down?" he asked.

I shook my head. "I've been having dull cramps all day long, but they get worse when I move. But this, this is like sharp jabs like I'm being stabbed in the stomach. Ow! Oh my God, it really hurts!" I winced in pain and suddenly started to feel dizzy.

"River, are you okay?"

"M—Mav, get me to the hospital. I feel like I'm going to die," I said, before I collapsed in his arms.

Mav

Hard rain skydived out of the clouds as I ran to place River in the passenger seat. I ran back to my side, trying to dodge as many oversized raindrops as I could, before pulling off. My tires swooshed against the wet city streets as I sped all the way to the hospital. The rain continued to fall out of the slate gray sky harder and faster until it almost became too hard to see a foot in front of me.

I hadn't remembered it raining that hard since the night of Luca's accident, nor had I stepped into a hospital since. The cold steel, automatic doors slid open as I carried River through to the emergency room, cradled in my arms. My eyes grazed over the seats in the waiting room overflowing with people with ailments that ranged from broken bones to heart attacks and pneumonia. I was happy the nurses didn't make us wait with everyone else. They wasted no time taking River back to start running tests and taking blood samples. Uneasiness rolled through my body like a dark wave. I couldn't stop pacing the floor as I waited for someone to come out and tell me what the fuck was going on.

Not knowing how long we'd be there, I arranged for Noemi to be with a sitter until we came home. I didn't like leaving Noemi with strangers, but I knew I couldn't leave River's side until I knew what the hell was going on.

HOURS LATER, River woke up after having to have emergency surgery. I was sitting in the well-worn visitors chair, listening to doctors and nurses tell us that her left fallopian tube had almost ruptured due to a tubal pregnancy. I searched her eyes for shock—anything to allude to the fact that she didn't know anything about being pregnant in the first place, but instead, I got the exact opposite.

Instead of shock, I got guilt.

Instead of denial, I got embarrassment.

Instead of sorrow, I got relief.

She'd known all along and kept it from me. I didn't know what to think.

EIGHT

River

I woke up to florescent lighting beaming in my face, which caused me to squint my eyes. I put my left hand over my eyes to shield them from the light as I slowly looked at my surroundings. There was a whiteboard with my name on it, the name of the nurse on shift, and the medication I was supposed to be getting. Boxes of gloves hung on the pale wall next to the metal IV stand with saline bags beside my bed. The smell of hand sanitizer and latex wafted past my nose as I glanced over to my left and saw Mav in the chair beside my bed.

I looked down at the automatic finger clip attached to my finger while silently trying to recall what exactly had landed me there in the first place. The only thing I remembered was utter pain. That's when the doctors and nurses came in to tell me that I'd suffered from an ectopic pregnancy and barely escaped with my life. Just the mere mention of death had my head spinning. I was ashamed, heartbroken, and relieved all at once. All I could do was chalk my loss up to a blessing in disguise, no matter how tragic it was. Unable to make eye contact with him or focus on the big medical terms the doctor was spewing out, my eyes bounced from the pale walls to the entangled monitoring wires and landed on the pulse clip clamped to my finger once more. The blood pressure cuff squeezing my arm until it went numb and then letting up again was the only thing that brought my thoughts back to alignment.

"So, what are you saying?" I asked the doctor.

"I'm saying that it may be hard for you to have a normal pregnancy if you decide to get pregnant again in the future. You may want to consider talking to a fertility specialist when you're ready. Whatever the case, you'll want to give your body at least a few months to make sure everything heals properly.

He may as well have been speaking Chinese to me because I didn't understand anything coming out of his mouth. “Can I get pregnant again?” I asked.

His head tilted to the side. “It’s not impossible, but I wouldn’t be doing my job if I didn’t tell you that another pregnancy does raise your risk of having this happen again. I’ll leave you two to be alone now. Please let me know if you have any more questions, Miss Newman, and take care.”

“Thank you, doctor.”

The door closed behind him, and I could no longer avoid having the conversation I had been dreading ever since the stick turned pink. My stomach was all knotted together as I stared down at my feet. I could barely look at him. I didn’t know how to feel or how to react to any of the news that had come my way within a matter of minutes. My nerves had my hands shaking uncontrollably as I slowly turned my eyes to Mav’s. The disappointment in his eyes alone made tears explode out of my eyes. I covered my face with my hands, unable to stop crying if I wanted to. All I wanted was for him to envelop me in his arms and tell me everything would be okay, but shit like that only happened in the movies.

I hadn’t had a chance to really process my own feelings, let alone expect for him to process his. I had no idea what I was going to say to him, or what he would have to say to me, but I knew the only choice I had was to come clean about everything and put it all out in the open. I kicked myself for not telling him the truth about the pregnancy in the first place. I had my reasons for keeping my own secret, but none of that seemed to matter anymore. I didn't know if he was ever going to see that I had true intentions by doing what I did. I would probably take a long time before he would be able to fully erase the pain and embarrassment I'd caused him and our relationship.

"Mav…" I said, trying to stop myself from melting into another puddle of tears.

I tracked his gaze down to my empty stomach. "I know it wasn't mine, so…"

"Yeah, it was Leander's baby…"

"So, you knew?"

I nodded instead of answering verbally.

"And you didn't tell me?" he continued.

"I didn't know how to."

"I don't have time not to trust you right now, aight? I already got too much shit on my plate."

"I'm sorry my unexpected pregnancy is such a burden on you when I'm the one sitting in a hospital bed!"

His jaw tightened as he sighed. "Does he know?"

I shook my head while responding, "No. I never told

him."

"Were you going to?"

"Does it matter now?" I replied.

"It does."

"I was, but only because I felt like he deserved to know."

He scoffed. "So, you were going to keep it and somehow make me think it was mine? Now, I see why you and your girl were thick as fuckin' thieves."

"Excuse me? I still didn't know what I was going to do, okay?" I admitted.

"Well, looks like God went ahead and made it easy for you."

My mouth hung open as my heart shattered. "Mav..."

"Sorry for your loss, River," he said before walking out.

I let out a heavy sigh as my chest trembled. I couldn't believe him. Every limb on my body felt as if it weighed one hundred pounds. I could barely lift my arm to wipe away the fresh tears clouding in my eyes. That was it;

Mav and I were through.

Mav

Anger and disappointment clouded my features. I felt defeated; played, even. I couldn't fuckin' believe it. It felt like I was in the middle of a bad dream that I couldn't wake up from. I didn't know what my next move was going to be, all I knew was that I had to get out of there. The woman I loved had just lost a child that wasn't mine and never told me about it. If there was one thing I hated, it was a lying ass female. Second chances weren't my thing. I really did love River, but the news about an illegitimate baby was enough to send a rift through any foundation, no matter how solid it seemed. It was the first time it felt like loving her was like fighting an uphill battle that I was sure I'd never win.

I thought the day that River told me that she was pregnant would be one of the happiest days of my life, but it wasn't. It had completely thrown me for a loop. We hadn't even gotten the opportunity to talk about having children outside of raising Noemi when she turned up pregnant by another nigga. It was as if my worst nightmare had come true. A part of me knew I should've turned the car around, headed back to the hospital, and reconciled things with her, but I didn't. I just couldn't face her knowing she'd hid information about another man's baby growing inside of her when she was supposed to be mine.

THE MOMENT I stepped into the pool hall, I smelled the scents of Black & Mild and Cuban cigar smoke congesting the air. I walked past all of the various pool tables covered in green or red felt until making my way to the very back of the hall where Sosa was standing with a stick in his hand.

"Sup?" he said, reaching out to dap me up.

"Yo."

"Why you got such a sour look on your face?"

Instead of replying, I shook my head to simply let him know I didn't want to talk about it. I watched as he split the triangle of balls with a loud crack, sending them spiraling across the table, while I was still trying to compartmentalize the news of River's pregnancy and her losing the baby the way that she did. As much as I needed someone to confide in, I had other things to discuss with him first.

"There's something I need to talk to you about," I said.

"What?"

I turned to face him. The two of us stood in silence for a few seconds, just listening to the balls crack against one another as they rolled across the table. "I know it's more than clear by now, but after I handle this nigga, I'm done…with everything."

I wanted to make it clear that as soon as that nigga was six feet in the ground, my job was done, and I would finally be able to wash my hands of the entire situation.

"If you would've said that to me years ago, I would've said I didn't see you doing it," he said while shaking his head, "but with everything that's going on, I get it."

"You know I've been seeing shit through a different lens for a minute. My goal when I got out was to go legit with my tattoo shop and shit. I wanted Luca to keep it going, but when he died, I thought I may have to give up on my dream and go back into the street, but now…"

"Say less, I respect it. You gotta do what you gotta do for your family, you know?"

"You know all this shit has an expiration date on it. I'm just not tryin' to burn out before then, and I'm for damn sure not going back to jail. Noemi already lost so much. She deserves to have someone around that's gon' live long enough to see them grow up and have they own kids."

"And that's why you'll always be a better mothafucka than me and the rest of us out here," he said.

"That's not all."

"What else is there?" he asked.

"I want you to take my place."

He tilted his head to the side in confusion. "I'm not a Malone."

"You're the closest thing to it. Don't worry, I've talked shit over with Salt. You've proven yourself ten times over, and he considers you to be family just as much as me."

"I just got one question," he said before lifting his drink to his lips.

"What?"

"I know you got your shop and shit, and your girl and all, but do you really think you'll be able to wipe away over years of street shit overnight just because you wake up and decide you wanna be a better nigga than the one you were yesterday?"

"I ain't say it was gon' be easy, aight?" I grimaced.

He took a step back and nodded. "Facts."

He was a grown ass man, and as my right-hand, he couldn't do anything but respect my decision. Even the slightest mention of River brought her right back to the forefront of my mind. I was tired of holding in my thoughts about everything that had just gone down, and who better to express myself with than Sosa? I knew he'd never tell a soul.

"Speaking of River, she's in the hospital," I blurted out.

"Then what the fuck you doin' here, nigga?"

"I just left…she was pregnant and lost the baby."

His eyebrows raised toward his forehead before he lowered his head. "I'm sorry, bro."

I shook my head. "It wasn't my baby, Sos."

I watched his face scrunch up. "What the fuck?"

"She was pregnant from the other nigga she was going to marry. It's not even the fact that she was pregnant by somebody else because I get that she was going to be with the nigga or whatever, but it's the fact that she never told me about it. She knew, and she kept it from me."

"Damn."

"Yeah, so now I don't know if I can trust her, and if I can't trust her, I don't need her around me. The only thing that's keeping me from telling her ass to pack her shit is Noemi."

"I wasn't going to speak on it, but when I went by to check-in on the house after they tried to hem you up, she started asking me a lot of questions like did I know you had a thing with Suki before Luca came along or where you were that night. It was all suspect to me."

I cut my eyes at Sosa, who had a stern look on his face. As my second in command, he never had a problem telling me the truth, no matter how hard it was for me to hear it. "What did you tell her?"

"I told her it didn't matter where you were because you ain't have nothin' to do with the shit."

"Bet, yo, you want another drink? I'm about to go to the bar."

"Henny, straight."

I nodded. "Bet, I'll be right back."

I walked away with even more questions in my head about River. She told me about her questioning my motives, but I didn't think she'd go so far as to bring Sosa into it. One thing was for sure, she and I were going to have to talk one day, but not until I was ready. For now, she was on the backburner of my mind and my heart.

I came back with two drinks in my hand to see Sosa with his ear glued to his cell phone. Once he hung up, he looked at me. "What?"

"I'll be right back," he said, walking out of the establishment.

He came back minutes later and handed me a flash drive. "What is this?" I asked.

"I just got the information you asked for."

"Do you know what's on it?"

"Nah, I figured you'd want to be the first to see."

"Aight, bet. Thanks, I'll look into it later."

Sebastian

"Ooh fuck, baby, right there!" Lauren moaned as she bounced her ass back against my dick.

"Mmm, shit. That's right, throw that fuckin' ass back," I said, with my thumbs firmly pressed into the dimples on her back, "but don't stop tellin' me what the fuck you were saying."

She looked back at me with her mouth wide and lips formed into an o-shape. "Oooh, okay, okay. I was saying there—mmm, shit, there's a property over on third avenue, and a few others not too far away from the—shit, mmm, from the airport that are vacant," she said, trying her best to talk business while taking each long stroke.

I pulled her hair and rested one hand on her shoulder as my strokes quickened. "Mmm, yeah. Find out how much they're going for and put a bid in for me."

I humped her like a dog in heat until I nutted all over her back. After cleaning herself up, she walked out of the bathroom with her perky breasts jiggling with each step.

"So, you were serious about me putting in a bid? You don't want to see them first?"

"Doesn't matter the condition, I'll probably knock them down and rebuild from the ground up or completely renovate anyway."

"You already own a nightclub, restaurants, and strip malls around the city, what more could you want?"

"I want it all," I told her while tossing three stacks of money on the bed. "You should already know that."

"I'm starting to," she said, while fanning herself with the stacks of money.

"You know what else I want?"

"What? Some more nookie?" She smirked.

"Besides that."

"What is it?" she asked, while sliding her four-inch heels back onto her feet.

"I need you to do something for me and put those connections of yours to good use."

"Do you mind being a little more specific?"

"I need you to get me more information on Maverick Malone."

She sucked her teeth. "This again? I told you what I knew the last time. What is your obsession with him?"

"I'm far from fuckin' obsessed, aight?"

"Could've fooled me," she mumbled.

I drew back my hand and struck her across her face, leaving a scolding red mark. "I told you I'm not fuckin' obsessed, and I meant that shit! Stop fuckin' playin' with me, bitch!"

She looked at me with horror in her eyes, and I swear I could see every hair on her arm raised in fear.

"You're going to do any and everything I tell you to

do when I tell you to do it, aight?" I warned.

She quickly bobbed her head as tears ran down her face. "O—okay, just please don't hit me again!"

"You'll never have to worry about me laying another hand on you again as long as you give me what I want."

"Okay," she nodded, "I'll ask around and see if I can find out anything else out."

"That's a good girl," I said, stroking her swollen cheek.

LATER THAT DAY, I was out getting gas when a car pulled up at the pump next to mine. I glanced up and noticed a kid in the backseat with her eyes glued to a tablet. A few seconds later, she looked up at me and smiled. I'd seen that smile before, but I couldn't figure out where. Puzzled, I got back in my car and started the engine. Before pulling off, I glanced back over to the little girl one more time and remembered where I'd seen her before. She was the same girl I'd seen on Suki's lock screen.

Although Suki mentioned having a daughter named Noemi, she never brought her around me or talked about her nonstop when we were together. I pulled over into a parking spot and watched the car through my rearview mirror. There was another woman with her that I'd never seen before. I waited until she got back in the car and pulled off before following behind them. I made sure to keep my distance as I followed them for a few miles until they parked and went to a nearby park. I parked and got out, wanting to get closer to see if she was really who I thought she was or not.

Hand-in-hand, they walked over to a grassy area with a bunch of little mothafuckas chasing each other around and screaming. I noticed the tablet fall out of her bag and jogged over to pick it up.

"Excuse me, I think you dropped this," I said, approaching the two of them.

They both turned to face me at the same time. "Oh, yeah that's her tablet. Noemi, remember you have to zip up your bookbag, so you don't lose your stuff," the woman said, grabbing the tablet from me and handing it to the girl.

"What do you say?"

"Thank you," she said, looking up at me.

"You're welcome, Noemi. You're beautiful just like your mother," I said, flashing a smile at the woman.

She smiled back and then shook her head. "Oh, I'm not her, uh, mom. But thank you."

"My fault, I didn't mean to offend."

"My mommy died," Noemi said, looking at me with

doe eyes.

My face went blank. "Oh, I'm sorry."

"No, no worries. You couldn't have known," the woman interjected.

"I shouldn't have assumed. I mean, I don't know what it's like to lose a mother, but I lost a kid once..."

I watched the light in her face dim before she responded, "We ought to be going now before all the swings are taken. Thanks for returning her tablet," she said before turning to walk away.

"Hold up, I uh, I don't usually do this, but I'd hate myself if I let the moment pass without telling you how beautiful you are. I would be honored if you let me take you out for a drink or dinner sometime."

She blushed. "Thank you, I'm flattered, but I'm—"

"Let me guess, you're taken."

"Yeah, something like that," she replied, head bobbing up and down.

"Well, maybe I won't feel like so much of a sucker if you took my card anyway. You don't have to use it, just hold onto it and maybe when you figure out your relationship status, you can give me a call," I said, reaching into my wallet and handing her a business card with the name of my club across the front.

She hesitated for a few seconds but took it and shoved it inside her purse. "Thanks, bye."

The little girl waved. "Bye."

"Bye, Noemi," I said, waving back.

I turned and headed back to my car with a smile on my face. Suki may not have told me where my money was before she died, but I was sure her daughter or that woman were the missing key I'd been looking for. I pulled out my phone and texted Lauren.

Me: [3:47 p.m.]: *Did Malone ever mention a kid?*

Lauren: [3:52 p.m.]: *Not that I recall, why?*

Me: [3:53 p.m.]: *Find out.*

Lauren: [3:55 p.m.]: *I think I remember seeing some toys when I went to his house when we first started working together.*

Me: [3:56 p.m.]: *Girl or boy?*

Lauren: [3:57 p.m.]: *Girl.*

I smiled. She'd been in his house, which meant she knew where he lived. She also confirmed that the little girl was related to him and somehow that woman she was with may have been too.

Me: [3:58 p.m.]: *Get the full layout of that nigga's house and send it to me.*

Lauren: [4:00 p.m.]: *Okay.*

River

My heart was completely broken over Mav's reaction to my miscarriage. The emptiness I felt inside hadn't subsided, and the pain hadn't eased as the days went by. He'd made it clear that things were over between us. His actions had left a sour taste in my mouth, and I'd gone back to sleeping upstairs in my old room to give him space on the off chance that he was home and not at the shop. When he was forced to be around me, we didn't speak. With my home life in shambles, it became a struggle just to pull myself out of bed and go in to work, but I knew if I'd stayed cooped up in the house, I'd eventually let my thoughts eat me alive and drive me crazy.

After over a week of not speaking, I knew I was going to have to make some changes.

It was cold and lonely living in the back of his mind, and I couldn't take it anymore. I didn't deserve it. A few days before I was scheduled to go back to work, I decided to go out and look at some new apartments around the city. I had no knowledge of how long he'd be cold to me, but if it came down to it, I knew I couldn't stay in his home forever. If it wasn't for Noemi, I'm sure he would've kicked my ass out long ago.

I had tried to forget everything about him, but completely stopping myself from loving every part of Mav would never be that easy. He had been inside of me, coursing through my veins. He'd made it clear that he couldn't be there for me at my lowest, so it was best that I cut and bled every drop of Maverick Malone out of my system until I was either free or dead.

For the rest of the day, I tried to keep busy by watching Netflix series and drinking wine; anything to keep me from crying again. I'd finally gotten some time to fold my laundry and was putting some washcloths and towels away underneath the bathroom sink when the locket Suki had given me hit the bathroom floor and popped open. I bent down to pick it up and saw a small USB flash drive inside.

"What the hell is this?" I muttered.

I put the rest of the towels away and went to grab my laptop to see what was on the drive. When the window opened, there was only one file on it.

32009 11th Street NE

Ask for Sung Zhang

Passcode: 003075

I grabbed my phone to take a picture of it and ejected the drive to place it back inside the locket.

AFTER WORK THE NEXT DAY, I typed the address into my phone and pulled up at Ameris Bank. I anxiously walked up to the counter, not knowing what the hell was going on.

"Hi, how can I help you today, ma'am?" the teller asked.

"H—hi. I'm um, looking for someone by the name of Sung Zhang…is he…or she here?"

"What is your name, ma'am?"

"River Newman."

"One second, please," she said before tapping a few buttons on her phone and putting the receiver up to her ear.

"Hi, Mr. Zhang, there's a woman by the name of River Newman here to see you…yes sir. Okay, I will, thank you."

She hung up the phone and looked back at me through the plexiglass separating us. "Mr. Zhang will be down in a minute to get you. Please wait over by the elevator doors," she instructed.

I bobbed a cautious nod before following her instructions. A couple minutes later, the elevator dinged and out walked a short Asian man with salt and pepper hair. "Miss Newman?"

"Yes." I nodded.

He outstretched his hand to shake mine. "Hello, I'm Sung Zhang. I'm the portfolio manager for your accounts."

"Accounts? What accounts?" I quizzed.

"Please, follow me and allow me to explain."

We got back on the elevator and went to the top floor and then into his office. He took a seat behind his large cherry wood desk and started typing at his keyboard.

"Can you please give me the passcode?" he asked.

"Oh, yes. It's um, wait one second," I said, pulling out my phone, "it's um, 003075."

"Thank you for verifying, Miss Newman," he said

before turning the computer screen around. "These are the current balances in your offshore savings accounts, gaining interest by the day."

"W—what is this?" I asked, looking at a bunch of numbers.

"You have sole ownership over these two accounts, one of your own and the other over a minor, Noemi Malone, until she comes of age. Both accounts combined are currently totaling at three million, five-hundred and sixty-two thousand dollars and forty-seven cents."

"Oh shit," I mumbled before clasping my hand over my lips. I'd found the money. All the fuckin' money.

"Yes, and as I said, these accounts are gaining significant interest by the day."

"What are these other numbers here?" I asked, pointing to the screen.

"Five percent of your money is automatically being invested into various types of cryptocurrency stocks. These numbers are your return."

My eyes tore away from the screen when I felt my phone vibrating in my purse. I pulled it out to see Mav's name written across the screen, but I was too much at a loss for words to answer. I slid it back inside my purse and placed my palms flat against my thighs.

"I—I don't know what to say."

"This is also for you," he said, reaching inside his desk and handing me a key to a safety deposit box. "I'll show you where it's located."

I followed him to another floor and into the room filled with walls of boxes, stopping at Box 911. "Is this it?"

"Yes, I will give you your privacy. I'll be just outside if you need me."

"Thank you."

I opened the box and pulled out a manilla envelope. Inside were two passports with both my picture and Noemi's with two totally different names, a red lighter, and a folded letter. "What the fuck..." I mumbled while unfolding the paper.

River,

If you're reading this right now, then that means...well, you know. I don't know what you know or how much, but just know everything I did was for a reason. Please don't be sad or mad at me or my decisions. I know you have a lot of unanswered questions, which will lead you to assume that you don't know me, but you do. I am still the girl that would sit around with you when we were seven years old, planning our double weddings and playing M.A.S.H.

Don't think that I've resorted to this just because of greed or boredom. I love my life, but I know the shit that comes with it, and I always wanted better for Noemi. She deserves a life that doesn't involve death notes and jail sentences just because of her last name, and I've made some mistakes trying to free her of that. I mixed and mingled with the right crowd for the wrong reasons, or the wrong crowd for the right reasons. Over time, the lines got blurred, and I did some things I'm not proud of. There's a part of me that does want to tell you everything from the beginning, but I think some secrets are better left untold. So, if more answers are what you want, I'm sorry I can't give you that.

I'm not perfect, and I didn't mean for things to go down like this, but this is me trying to make it right. Luca taught me the game, and I made it work for all of us. Nothing I've done will trace back to you. The money and these passports are your safety net, River. If things get as bad as I fear they will, take Noemi and go as far away as you can.

I just need you to promise me three things. One, is that you'll be careful. Two, is that you'll raise my daughter as your own. Three, is that you'll burn this after reading. Thank you for being the mother to Noemi that I couldn't' be. I'm sorry, and I love you always.

-Su

Tears poured out of my eyes like water bursting through a dam as I folded the note back into its original creases. I slid everything back into the envelope, shoved it inside my purse, and quickly headed back to the parking garage. The moment my car door slammed, I burst into a full meltdown as I thought back to one of our last conversations.

"So, where we going?" I asked, feeling myself light up for the first time in days.

"Hmm, somewhere sexy, you know? We can't go nowhere basic that any fuckin' body can go to. I'm thinking...the Maldives or St. Barts. Yeah, St. Barts, it's settled!"

I shrugged lazily. "I don't even know where that is."

"It doesn't matter because we're going! We'll book the tickets tomorrow!"

"Wait, are you serious?"

"Yes! You're my best friend!" she said, hooking her arm in mine.

"Luca is gon' be fine with you whisking me off on an expensive girl's trip?"

"Girl, please. The pussy is the key to everything. Plus, if he ever had a problem with it, I've got my own money. Trust, I can afford it."

My forehead creased. "Since when did you start working?" I asked, shocked at the news that my best friend had actually gone out and got a job.

"Don't try to play me, bitch! I make things happen when I need to make things happen, aight? A bitch is always thinkin' about her next move."

I sighed while gripping the steering wheel. Suki had made it clear she had to have the last laugh even from the grave. I'd never known her to think so many steps ahead, but it was clear that she had traces of finesse and hustle laced in her DNA. Mav did say that Luca was the king of moving money around. If he taught Suki how to do what he did, then she was smarter than I'd ever given her credit for. Somehow, she'd managed to get into that man's account, move his money, and by the time he realized it was gone, it was already moved offshore, invested, and making thousands of dollars by the day—making way for her own posthumous pay day for Noemi and me. I guess it was true that you can never truly know a person, no matter how close you think you are.

Before pulling off, I took the letter and lighter out of my purse and walked over to the nearest trashcan to honor one of her dying wishes. The lighter flicked, igniting the flame. I held it to the edge of the loose-leaf paper and watched it instantly turn brown and begin to disintegrate.

"I love you too," I mumbled, watching the ashes fall into the trash.

Mav

I was still indecisive about my feelings for River after finding out about her miscarriage and the pregnancy she hid from me. I'd be lying if I said there wasn't a part of me that didn't see her as tainted. Initially, it seemed like her and Suki were two sides of the same fuckin' coin, and I didn't have time for liars and scheming ass bitches in my life. I needed space to sort out my own shit and get over myself. It took some time, but I had finally realized the error of my ways and how much I'd taken River for granted. The truth was, if the shoe was on the other foot and I had a baby on the way with someone who wasn't her, I wouldn't know how to tell her either. At the end of the day, there was already enough coldness in the world, and River didn't deserve mine. When she didn't answer my call, I decided to text her.

Me [4:17 p.m.]: *Do you have plans tonight? I was hoping we could talk over dinner.*

River [4:21 p.m.]: *Dinner? What about Noemi?*

Me [4:22 p.m.]: *I'll get a sitter.*

I WAS DOWN AT MY SHOP when Lauren walked through the front door. She flashed me her bright, wide smile and started walking my way.

"Hey there, stranger." She cheesed.

"Hey yourself," I told her, "what you doin' down here?"

"I always check in on clients after a sale just to see how business is doing, and to let special clients like you know I'm available if you're interested in a...*showing*."

I smirked. "Business is good, and no thank you."

"I should get a tat while I'm here, huh," she said, looking around.

"You ever been tatted before?"

"Oh, you mean to tell me you don't remember that butterfly on the inside of my...never mind," she said, fluttering her eyes my way.

"Yo, you somethin' else."

She winked. "Well, I'll get out of your hair. It was good seeing you again, Mav. Hopefully, it won't be too long before we can bump into each other again, maybe in a more intimate setting. I'm going to use your bathroom before I go."

"The bathroom is for paying customers only," I reminded her.

"I thought I paid you pretty well the last time, or did you need to step in here with me for a quick reminder?"

"Damn, girl. You don't stop, do you?" I asked, running my hand down my beard.

"What can I say? I go after what I want. I haven't heard you say you're in a relationship yet, so I'm going to keep shooting my shot."

"It's complicated."

"I can uncomplicate things…it's kind of my specialty as a *stress reliever*, remember?"

I bit my bottom lip. "Use my shit and get outta here before you start somethin' you can't finish."

She winked again. "Your loss."

She walked to the bathroom, and I pulled out my vibrating phone to read River's latest text.

River [4:47 p.m.]: *Okay.*

LATER THAT NIGHT, River and I were being seated in a private section in the back of the Japanese restaurant with our own private table and teppanyaki chef. She hadn't said more than two words to me on the way to the restaurant. Just by reading her body language, I could tell she was uncomfortable. It was as if everything I said to try and spark a conversation was followed by a pregnant pause. We'd gone from inseparable to complete strangers, and I had to man up and take the blame for putting a wedge between us. I locked eyes with her, noticing the fact that she still chose to wear red lipstick. I could barely drag my hawkish gaze away from her. Even through the brokenness on her face, she still looked more beautiful than ever under the ambient lighting.

"You look beautiful, River," I said.

"Thanks…you don't look so bad yourself."

"I'm aight." I shrugged.

"You don't see all those women staring at you like they wanted to take a bite out of you as we walked through the restaurant?"

"Ain't nobody else worth having my attention but you…and I just wanna say thank you."

"For what?"

"For agreeing to talk."

"I was beginning to think we never would again," she admitted.

"I know, and that's on me. That pregnancy shit threw me for a fuckin' loop, but I wasn't being a man about that shit. I let the way I felt about the shit turn me cold to you, and you didn't deserve it, so I want to apologize for that."

She flashed her tear-filled eyes up to mine. "Thank you for saying that…I really needed to hear that. I've been feeling so alone."

"I never should've left you to go through that shit alone, and I'll never do no shit like that to you again. You've got my word on that."

"I just never thought you'd play me like that."

"Play you? Is that what you think I did?"

"That's what I know you did, Mav. And I wanna know why, when all I've ever done is hold you down and help you out when you asked and even when you didn't. You sat there and listened to that doctor tell me that I may never be able to have kids again, and you shitted on me! On me! The woman you chased down and broke up a wedding for just to confess your fuckin' love for."

She was applying pressure, but she needed the release, and I needed to hear how she really felt. I knew I'd fucked up, but I didn't know how much I'd hurt her until I heard it from her own mouth. Having her put the mirror up to my face was a hard pill to swallow, but I appreciated her for staying true to how she felt and not backing down. Our conversation was interrupted by the waitress who delivered bottles of sake to our table and introduced us to our chef for the evening. We sat and watched the chef in silence as we sipped our drinks. I backed up from the large, hot flame while he prepared steak, lobster, shrimp, and chicken hibachi with vegetables and rice. Once our plates had been filled, we were back to being left alone.

River looked up from her plate. "Listen, Mav, you've apologized, and I receive that, but I'm going to ask you something, and I want a straight answer."

"Anything."

"Do you really love me? And before you answer, let me just say that I know the whole pregnancy situation was messy, okay? I get that. But the way you treated me…that's not what you do to someone that you love. You're supposed to stay and work it out. You're supposed to fight, to be there. And I get that learning to love the rose and the thorns in someone takes time, but after what you said and how you acted, I just don't know if you're capable of that. I mean, how do I know that the next time I'm going through something, you won't just up and leave me high and dry again?"

"River, I'm sorry, aight? And I know it's going to take more than words to show you that I mean that, but I'm here, and I'm willing to put in the work if you'll give me the chance. Anything you want me to do, I'll do it. And to answer your question, yes, I do love you, and I'm just—"

"A complicated, selfish ass mothafucka?" she asked, finishing my sentence.

A laugh made its way past my lips as I nodded.

"Yeah, exactly."

She flashed a genuine smile my way that made me feel warm inside. Her smiles were like home, and I couldn't go the rest of my life without seeing one on her face every day. As her man, it was my job to make sure that she never felt pain from me ever again.

"Now I have a question for you," I said.

"What?"

"Will you finally accept my gift?"

Her brows wrinkled in confusion. "What gift?"

"This," I said, pulling out the bracelet I'd originally given her for her birthday.

She grinned. "You never took it back?"

"No, I was hoping one day you'd want to wear it."

Instead of responding, she outstretched her arm, and I slid it over her tiny wrist to watch it sparkle even under the dim lighting.

"It really is beautiful," she said, admiring it with a smile.

"Not as beautiful as you."

RIVER AND I walked up to the front door and saw that it was open. When we walked in, the babysitter I'd hired was laying in the middle of the foyer in a puddle of her own blood.

River let out an ear-curdling scream. "Oh my God, Noemi! Where is Noemi?"

"U—upstairs."

She darted upstairs towards Noemi's room before I could grab her. I whipped out my phone to call 9-1-1 and my gun simultaneously. "Is anyone else still in the house? How many of them were there?" I asked, scanning everything in my immediate sight.

She outstretched her trembling bloody hand to mine. "Please don't let me die. I—I don't wanna die."

I glanced down at her wounds. She'd been stabbed in the stomach and wasn't going to live long enough to see the inside of an operating room. "Just hold on, you're gonna be okay. Everything is gonna be okay, aight? I just need you to tell me who did this to you," I said, trying to ease her mind of the inevitable.

"I—I don't know. They just s—s—said…"

"What? What did they say?"

"That this w—was a warning."

My blood boiled as I held her trembling hand in mine and felt the life leave her body. "Fuck!" I roared.

After calling 9-1-1, I shot Sosa a text to let him know it was time to apply pressure. If he was going to take a shot at the king, he should've made sure he killed me. By the time the cops arrived and took our statements, River and I were spent. My house had been ransacked, the babysitter had been stabbed in the stomach, and Noemi had slept through the entire thing.

"Who the fuck would do this? She was just a fuckin' neighborhood kid," I said, finishing the liquor in my glass.

River refilled my glass without saying a word, and I glanced up at her, thanking her with a nod.

"How's Noemi?" I asked.

"She's fine, still fast asleep with the TV on."

"I swear that kid would sleep through an earthquake if we let her."

"That's a good thing, at least tonight," she said.

"Come here," I said, pulling her into my arms and nestling my head against the side of her neck.

“This shit is getting out of hand, Mav. I know when you first told me what you wanted to do I was against it, but I’m scared.”

“I’m gon’ handle it, soon. I’ve been taking my time, tryna make all the right moves, but this is another level. We need to bulk up security. I’ll have people here first thing in the morning. Until then, you and Noemi don’t leave the house.”

She turned to look at me with a look of disapproval. “I have to go to work, Mav. I can’t stay cooped up in the house like Fort Knox, and Noemi still has school, too.”

“So? Quit your fuckin’ job, River. You don’t need that shit anyway, and you can homeschool her if you want.”

“Listen to yourself, you sound crazy.”

“No, you listen to me. You don’t know the game like I do. Niggas are testing me left and right, and I can’t risking losing Noemi or you.”

“Did the babysitter say anything to you before she…”

“She said they told her that this was a warning. The way those mothafuckas ran through here, I know they were looking for someone.”

“Or something…and I think I know what,” she

admitted.

My forehead creased. "What do you know, River?"

She sighed and got up to fully face me. I watched her pop open the locket around her neck and point inside. "You see this?"

"The fuck is that?"

"It's a flash drive. Suki left it for me."

"What's on it?"

"A passcode to offshore accounts with over three million dollars in it."

My eyes widened. "You found the fuckin' money?"

She bobbed her head. "She left it to me…and Noemi. Along with a note and two passports with new identities for me and her if things got bad. At first I thought she was being a little too overly cautious, but after what happened here tonight, I—I don't know what to think."

"When did you find all this out?"

"Earlier today. That's where I was when you called me, and I didn't answer."

"You said she left a note? What did it say? Did she

leave a name?"

River shook her head. "No. She said that everything she did was because she was trying to give Noemi the life she deserved, which was one that wasn't tied to her last name and all that came with it…that's why she was doing all that she was doing to get money."

"Was she planning to run off with Noemi or something?"

"I don't think so. I just think she got too caught up and saw that everything was about to blow up right in her face seconds before the bomb went off."

I pressed my lips together tight and sighed. Given the decisions my own father made in order to give Luca and I a better life, I could understand why Suki wanted the same for Noemi. I just didn't know why she had to sell her body to do it. But I guess it wasn't for me to understand.

"You still got the note?" I asked.

"No. It's gone, I burned it."

I took another gulp of my drink. Even from the grave, Suki's past had put everyone's future at stake, leaving me to tie up her loose ends. I would do whatever I had to do to make sure Noemi and River were good, whether I was around or not.

River

I was in the kitchen cooking breakfast for the three of us while Noemi sat at the kitchen island watching *Butterbean's Café* on her tablet and sipping a cup of orange juice. It had been a few days since the break in, and I was trying my best to make things seem as normal as possible for Noemi, and not like I was really walking on eggshells and looking over my shoulder every three seconds. Mav had the security system bulked up as promised, but I would still feel hair raise on my arm like a scared cat whenever I heard anything go bump in the night.

"Where's Uncle Mav?" Noemi asked, popping her head up.

"Uh, I think he's getting dressed. He's got some work stuff to do down at his tattoo shop."

"But he said he would take me to get ice cream," she pouted.

"Noemi, it's ten o'clock in the morning. You have all day to get ice cream," I assured her.

"I'm going to get a tattoo one day and be like Uncle Mav."

"Oh, yeah? What are you gonna get?"

She cheesed. "Barbie," she said, feeling confident in her response.

An innocent laugh broke past my lips. "Barbie, huh?"

"Yup."

"Yo, where are your keys?" Mav asked, popping his head into the kitchen. "I'm going to move your car into the garage."

"In my purse I think. It's over on the table," I said, pointing to it, "just grab them."

Mav walked over and fished around until he pulled out my jingling keys in his hand and a card with it. "What's this?”

I looked at it and immediately kicked myself for not throwing it in the trash when I had the chance. I hadn’t bothered to even look at the card given to me by the man at the park when he returned Noemi’s tablet. “It’s nothing.”

“Don’t look like nothin’. How the fuck do you know Sebastian Keyes?”

“Lower your voice and watch your mouth,” I said, tilting my head in Noemi’s direction.

Mav pulled me into the living room with a stern look on his face. “Where the fuck did you get this card, River? And don’t lie to me.”

“Some man in the park gave it to me when Noemi dropped her tablet. I swear, I forgot it was in there. I only took it to be nice.”

“When was this?”

“A little over a week ago maybe,” I said, wracking my brain to recall as many details as I could.

“What did he look like?”

“Um, light-skinned, bald head, beard. I think he was wearing a gold chain around his neck. I remember thinking it looked expensive, but that was it.”

"What did he say to you?"

"Noemi dropped her tablet and he caught up to us and gave it back, that's all. I mean, he did tell me I was beautiful and told Noemi that she was as beautiful as her mother, assuming that was me."

"Man, fuck!" Mav roared before he started pacing the floor.

"What? Who is Sebastian Keyes?

Mav let out a sharp breath and shook his head. "Fuck! I had a feeling, but I couldn't be sure until now. He's the one who killed Luca and Suki, River."

My forehead creased as my heartrate started to quicken. "What? How can you be so sure? What does he have to do with any of it?"

"Go get Suki's phone," he told me.

I darted into our room and grabbed the phone from my underwear drawer and turned it on. The two of us stood and watched the video clip and listened to the voicemails again. I hadn't touched the phone in weeks, let alone listened to the voicemails. As soon as I heard his voice, I felt foolish for not connecting the dots sooner.

"He's the fuckin' man in the video, River. This mothafucka was doing business with Luca all the while fucking his wife. She took his money and obviously, he tried to get her back by exposing her to Luca since he had access to him."

"And when he didn't get the money back, he killed them both," I said, finishing his sentence.

"Yeah."

"Oh, my God…" I said, before clasping my hand over my mouth.

"What?"

"Noemi. She—she told him that her mother died after I told him that I wasn't her mother. What if he followed me here? What if I led him straight to us? What if he knows I have the money and tries to come back and hurt me and Noemi?"

My heart raced with anxiety and fear as I thought about all the scary plausible possibilities. All I wanted to do was stay in our safe little bubble for as long as we could, but that was no longer on the table. I had no idea what that man was capable of, and I didn't want to find out what he was going to do next.

"Mav, I can't believe I'm saying this, but…I need for you to make all this go away. I need you to kill him, for me and Noemi."

"Don't worry about it. I'm definitely going to handle

this mothafucka," he assured me before his phone rang.

After a two-minute conversation, he turned back to face me. "I gotta go."

"What happened? Who was that?" I asked, panic raging through my voice.

"One of my artists down at the shop. He said there's a health inspector there. I gotta go meet him.

I nodded slowly. "Okay. Be safe."

"Don't worry, I will."

Mav

I'd never expected to hear River ask me to kill someone, but fear changed people. I pushed my thoughts of revenge to the side to focus on the task at hand, making sure I crossed all my T's and dotted my I's for the inspector. When I walked into the shop, my eyes landed on a pasty white woman with glasses pushed on top of her forehead and a clipboard in her hand.

"Mr. Malone?"

"Yes."

"Good morning, I'm Rebecca Stevens. I've been assigned to inspect your business due to a formal complaint that was filed at my office."

I frowned. "A complaint? What kind of complaint?" I asked. I kept my shit tight, so there had never been a cause for concern.

"I'm not at liberty to discuss that information right now, sir."

"Why not? I'm the business owner. You should be able to disclose any information about my business to me."

I watched as she shifted her weight from one leg to the other, instantly becoming unraveled. Something told me that my random visit wasn't so random after all. That nigga was trying to come for my business. He probably figured if he couldn't manage to take me down in the streets, getting my business shut down would be his backup plan. The universe was trying its hardest to take me down, but I wasn't going to fold.

"What health department did you say you worked for again?" I asked.

"I, err—I uh," she stammered.

"How much did he pay you?"

Her shoulder flinched. "W—what?"

"You heard what the fuck I said!"

"Five hundred dollars," she confessed.

"Five hundred dollars? Do you know who you're fuckin' with just to get five-hundred fuckin' dollars?"

"I—I'm sorry, sir. I was just supposed to come in and find some drugs."

"Drugs? Why the fuck would there be drugs in my fuckin' shop?"

"I—I don't know!" she said, shaking with fear.

"Where were you supposed to find these drugs?" I asked, steepling my long fingers together.

"In the w—women's bathroom, behind the trashcan."

"C'mon, let's go see what you find."

I walked behind her as she stepped into the bathroom and walked straight over to reveal a small packet of cocaine right underneath the trashcan as she said.

"Mothafucka!"

"I—I'm sorry, sir. I—I."

"Take that shit and get the fuck outta my shop. I swear to God if I see you around me or my shit ever again, I won't be so nice."

She quickly scurried past me and left. I shook my head, mad as fuck that someone had tried to plant drugs in my shit. I thought back, running different days and scenarios through my mind until I stopped on Lauren's random ass visit. She asked to use the bathroom and was sure to scurry out right after. It had to have been her, I just didn't know why. I was going to have to make sure I paid her ass a visit.

ON MY WAY back home, my lawyer called. I'd been letting him work things out on his end while I focused on other shit, but I was happy to get an update.

"It's been a minute, Joel. You got good news for me, right?" I answered.

"I do. So, it seems like the case they're trying to build is falling apart at the seams. The two agents that were interrogating you that day have officially been reassigned."

"So that's it, right? I'm good?"

"Not quite. There's still the matter of your cell phone pinging close to the scene. I know I've asked you this before, but are you sure there isn't anything you can tell me or anyone I can reach out to that can validate where you were the night of the accident?"

I still had Suki's phone, but I couldn't give it up until Sebastian was taken care of. "Nah."

"Then, can you at least tell me where you were? We have lawyer, client privilege. I can't tell anyone, but it would make my job a lot easier if you told me the truth."

I sighed, recalling that night in my memories. Luca and I had been on the phone arguing about business matters, and I hung up seconds prior to his accident. The words said in that call haunted me every night as I thought about them being the last thing he heard before he took his last breath. Even though I wasn't involved in his accident, nobody knew that I blamed myself for his death.

"I was on the phone with him, driving through town. I'd been trying to get in touch with him all night, but he'd been ignoring me—talkin' about he was spending time with his wife and shit. I didn't get the importance of it at the time, but I do now. We argued. We both said some things that we never should've said, and then he was gone. And I never got to apologize for the shit I said. I never got to make that right," I confessed.

He sighed. "Damn, I'm sorry, Maverick. I really am."

"That's my cross to bear, not yours."

"Okay. I'll keep working my end and you just keep your shit on the up and up."

I bobbed my head in silence, neglecting to tell him about the run-in with the fake ass health inspector and drugs in my shop.

AFTER I TOOK A SHOWER and got redressed, I headed down to the barbershop for a fresh cut. The music on the radio blared through the overhead speakers in the ceiling, trying to drown out the roaring sound of the clippers against the back of my neck. After my cut was done, my barber reclined the chair to shape up my beard and sideburns. I lay still while my eyes glanced over at the broom leaning against the wall and hair scattered across the floor. The door chimed, and my eyes landed on Lauren as she walked into the nail salon next door. My body instantly tensed, and my barber stopped to look at me.

"Yo, you aight, nigga?"

"Yeah, I'm good," I told him.

As soon as I was done, I exited the shop and saw her car parallel parked on the street. I got back in my truck and waited for her to come out of the salon. By the time she came out, the sun had started to set. After checking my surroundings, I ran up on her as she approached the driver's side door.

"Yo," I said.

She jumped when she saw me and then tried to cover up her nerves with a wide smile. "Mav? Hey. What's up?"

"This," I said, lifting my shirt to reveal the gun tucked in my jeans.

Her eyes widened with panic. "Mav—what—"

"Get in the fuckin' car," I demanded while walking over to the passenger side and getting in.

"I'm sorry!" she confessed, wrapping her freshly manicured hands around the steering wheel.

"You apologizing, and I ain't even said why I'm here yet, so get on the interstate and start fuckin' talkin'."

Small droplets of sweat started to gather across her forehead and upper lip as she followed my directions before saying another word. "I think I know why you're here."

"Oh yeah? And Why is that?"

"Sebastian…Sebastian Keyes," she mumbled.

"You've been workin' with this mothafucka the entire time?" I questioned.

"No. No! Not at first. We just got acquainted through work stuff—real estate. We only recently started to take things to the next level. Then, he just randomly started bringing you up every time we saw each other, digging for information."

"What kind of information?"

"Anything. He wanted to know everything about you. When I told his ass he sounded obsessed with you, he hit me! The nigga turned into Dr. Jekyll and Mr. Hyde on me in the blink of an eye. I was scared! I'm sorry, I don't know what he wants. He only told me he wanted to do business with you."

As she talked, her phone began to ring from inside her Birkin bag by my feet. I dug inside it to find Sebastian's name written across the screen with a picture of the two of them kissing. By the time she finished her sentence, the phone had stopped ringing. A couple seconds later, he called back. "Answer the phone, and I swear to God if you act fuckin' stupid, I'll blow your fuckin' brains out," I warned.

She bobbed her head, causing tears to fall out of her eyes. "H—hello?" she answered, while clearing her throat.

"Bitch, what the fuck did I tell you about not

answering the phone when I fuckin' call you the first time."

"I'm sorry, baby. I—I just got my nails done and my phone was in my purse. I'm driving."

"Where the fuck you going?" he asked.

She shot her eyes to me in search of an answer. When I shook my head, she had to quickly think on her toes. "I'm going a few counties over to meet with a potential client. You know the money never sleeps."

"Yeah, aight. Hit me up when you done."

"Okay, I will. Bye."

"So, the drugs at my shop and the phony ass health inspector, that was you?" I asked after I ended the call.

She nodded. "Yes. At first, I didn't think anything of it, and then his asks just kept getting more personal and weirder."

"What else did he ask you for?"

"The layout to your home. He was looking for something, but he wouldn't tell me what it was. I swear, that's all I know!"

"What did you get in return?"

"He threw a lot of extra bands my way at first, and like I said, then things got physical between us. Like I said, I didn't see the problem at first, but by the time I figured out something was really up, I was getting slapped around and threatened. I value my life, Maverick. And I'm sorry for putting you in harm's way, I should've come to you about it. That day at your shop, I—I wanted to warn you, but I was just too scared to say anything or what would happen to me if he found out."

I drew in a deep breath and then exhaled loudly. He'd run out of money and started paying her ass in D. She was pillow talking with the enemy, airing my dirty laundry for free.

"Does he know we fucked?" I questioned.

"No. I never told him that."

I glanced up at the road ahead just in time to have her take the next exit. "Pull over into the lot over to your left," I told her.

"W—where are we going?"

"Just keep driving this mothafucka."

I directed us to a junk yard and made her get out of the car and pop the trunk. We'd arrived at our destination, and I'd honestly heard enough. She was the last person I would suspect, but then again, I didn't put shit past anyone. As much as she claimed to be just an innocent pawn in the game, her hands were dirty too. If she'd never given him my layout or my address, the babysitter would've never lost her life. She was also brave enough to plant drugs at my shop, which could've gotten my entire dream taken away from me by giving the feds exactly what they needed to further build their case against me. Hell no, there was no remorse in my heart. Her ass had to die.

"Get the fuck out of the car and give me your phone," I demanded.

"Here, take it. Take whatever you want, just please don't kill me, Mav. I'm sorry! I didn't know what to do. Please forgive me!" she begged.

With my gun pressed to her back, she walked around to the back of the car. I reached back inside the car and popped the trunk. "Get in."

"W—what?"

"You heard what the fuck I said," I growled, cocking my gun.

Shaking like a leaf on a tree, she slowly climbed into her trunk and laid there. "Mav, p—please. Please, don't do this! I'll do whatever you want! If you want me to go to the police station and tell them everything I know I will. I swear, I will! I'll do anything you want, just p—"

"You put the people I love in harm. I can never forgive you for that," I told her.

In one swift motion, I put two bullets in her chest and watched her lifeless body fall backwards into the trunk. I looked at Lauren's body as dark crimson blood pooled around her mouth and nose.

"I need a pick up and a cleanup at the chop shop," I said into the receiver as soon as Sosa answered.

"Got it. I'm en route to you now."

Sosa's uncle owned the junkyard and chop shop that we were at. It came in handy for times such as this. I planned to have her car torn apart and sold for parts, as well as her body. Although things hadn't gone exactly as I'd planned, the job was done and that was all that really mattered to me.

"Bet."

I held Lauren's phone up to her lifeless body to unlock her phone and went straight to her call log. I pressed Sebastian's name and waited for him to pick up.

"Yeah?" he answered.

"You must have a death wish fuckin' with me, nigga," I growled, instantly feeling rage as soon as I heard his voice.

"Who the fuck is this?"

"Who the fuck you think it is, nigga? I want my money, tonight, or she dies," I warned, not telling him that Lauren had already been cancelled.

He scoffed. "You think I give a fuck about her? You'd just be doin' my dirty work for me."

"Money, tonight," I repeated.

"Time and place?"

"Stay by your phone," I said and ended the call.

I took a picture of his number with my phone and let hers fall to the ground. I stepped on it, crushing the screen into tiny little pieces under my shoe.

WHEN SOSA GOT to me, I got inside the car with him while his uncle's men handled Lauren's body and her car.

"Yo, it's going down tonight. I found out that nigga, Sebastian, from the club I told you to look into is behind everything."

"How'd you find out?"

"That's the reason for the pick-up. He was pumping information out of my real estate agent. The mothafucka was coming for my business, he was behind the break in at my crib, and I know he killed my brother. The mothafucka dies tonight!"

"Where do you want to set it up at?"

"I'ma take 'em to the trap."

Sosa shook his head. "Nah, you been through enough. You said it yourself you out the game and you need to keep your shit clean. Let me do this."

As much as I wanted to be there when he took his last breath, I knew Sosa had a point. I'd spent so many nights calculating and fantasizing about what I was going to do when I found the mothafucka that stole my brother from me. Now that the moment was in front of me, I was having a hard time letting go. I glanced down at my lock screen and looked at the picture of River and Noemi. They deserved to have me come home to them every night. I couldn't do that from behind bars. My Uncle Salt was right. As long as the mothafucka died, it didn't really matter who pulled the trigger.

"You sure?" I asked.

"I'm positive. You want me to take over, right? Get home to your girls, and I'll call you when it's done."

I nodded. "Just make sure you give 'em hell."

ELEVEN

Sebastian

After Lauren got the layout of Mav's home to me, I had my men ready to run all through his shit to find my money. I was livid when I found out that not only did they turn up with nothing, but they'd also caught a fuckin' body in the process, which meant I had to be the one to clean it up and make it all go away. I'd spent weeks trying to buy time until I could come up with some money, all while trying to find my own. After I got the phone call from Mav on Lauren's phone, I knew the shot clock had run out. I didn't have any more time to waste. An hour later, I got a text from an unknown number with the address and time.

I PULLED UP to a run-down trap house with colorful graffiti tags on the outside. There were high weeds growing wildly on the outside, and there was dim lighting shining through the window inside. I slung the navy blue duffel bag over my shoulder and tucked my gun inside my pants. I knew better than to show up without protection. I only had one thing in mind, to kill Maverick Malone and get the fuck out of there with my life. There would be no exchange of money from my hand to his. If he was smart, he'd tell me what I wanted to know about my own money. I picked a path through the rat feces and dead cockroaches and looked inside. There were empty liquor bottles on the ground and peeling paint on the walls with holes in them. The nigga with the dreads was sitting on an old couch, alone.

"What are you doing here? Where's Malone?" I asked as soon as I walked in.

He stood to his feet. "You know why I'm here. Where's the money?" he responded.

"What was your name again? Sosa?" I asked.

"Don't worry about what the fuck my name is. Where is the money?"

I smiled. "Relax. We're both friends here, right?"

"Wrong. I ain't come to talk or shoot the shit with you, nigga. I'll just take what I came for," he said, brandishing his gun.

"It's right here," I said, tossing the duffel on the

couch.

The moment he looked inside and realized there was no money in it, I whipped out my gun and put two bullets in his kneecaps.

"Ahhh! Fuck!" he screamed out in pain as he fell to the ground. "What the fuck!"

I reached down and yanked one of his dreads straight out of his head. His scalp started to puff up and bleed as he yelled.

"Where the fuck is my money?" I asked.

"What money? We don't owe you no money, nigga. You owe us!"

"You know exactly what money I'm talkin' about! Where's my three million?"

"Three million? I don't know shit about no three million dollars, mothafucka!"

"Look, I don't want to kill you. I know you're probably just an innocent bystander in all of this. You're not even the one I want. I really did think I was going to meet Maverick tonight. I'm highly disappointed."

"I just told you, I don't know shit about no money," he said, trying his best to reach for his gun.

I drew back and kicked him in the face, sending at least four of his teeth flying out of his mouth. He screamed out in pain.

The floor creaked underneath me every step I took. I walked into the kitchen and flipped on the lights. The cockroaches scattered back into the dark corners while dead flies laid on the countertops. The air was polluted with cigarette smoke and stale water. There were black mildew splotches and water stains above on the ceiling. I came back with a bottle of liquor in hand and turned it up to my lips before pouring the rest out on him while laughing.

"I bet you planned to come here, get the little money I owed you, and you were gon' kill me, right? It was gon' be easy, right? Face it, mothafucka! I'm faster than you. I'm more trained than you. I love it when a mothafucka underestimates me!" I cheered. "This is lightwork to me. Malone, now maybe that would've been a challenge, but then again, his brother wasn't."

"Wh—what?"

"Don't act like you don't know I was behind it. I know Malone has figured it out by now, but I bet he still doesn't know the whole story."

When he tried to slide his way across the floor, I leaned down and yanked out another dread from his scalp. "Ahhhh!"

"You ever had your heart broken? I imagine the pain you're feeling right now feels similar. Love is a crazy thing, ain't it?"

"What the fuck is wrong with you?"

"Did you know she was pregnant with my baby when I killed her? She told me as if it would make me change my mind after she tried to kill me and robbed me! I could never forgive that bitch for that."

The more he yelled, the more I realized he didn't know shit about my money. I refused to think it had vanished into thin air, but he was not going to be any help to me. I'd become bored with his screams and decided to put an end to my game of torture.

"Why the fuck are you tellin' me all of this, nigga?" he asked, crumpled over in agony.

"Because dead men tell no tales," I said, just before putting two bullets in his head.

My fingertip hugged the trigger as I fired two more bullets into his chest. Gun smoke oozed from the tip of my gun as I looked down at his dead body. I fished around in my pocket and pulled out a lighter before tossing the flame onto the leather couch. I watched the flame catch on and slowly spread throughout the house, burning away my existence as I made my exit. With no money, I had to figure out how I was going to get the fuck out of town before anyone got wind of it. I knew the moment Maverick found out I'd killed his friend, he'd send the dogs out on my ass.

River

I rolled over and tapped my screen to see what time it was. It was after one o'clock in the morning, and I was horny. It had been months since I'd been touched. Partly because I took my time healing, and partly because I didn't want to be. So much shit had been going down that I'd neglected my own carnal needs, but I needed the relief right then and there. I turned the TV volume up a few notches while reaching into my nightstand drawer to pull out my vibrator. After opening up a private web browser on my iPad, I searched through videos of one of my favorite amateur porn stars, *IssaNutBaby*. There was nothing super exciting about watching a man jack his own dick, no matter how big it was. That wasn't what turned me on. It was the dirty talk that came out of his mouth that sent me spiraling over the edge and wetting up the sheets. It wasn't until I'd been broken off by Maverick Malone that I realized how much I loved being talked dirty to.

So, whenever I was in the mood, listening to his deep sultry voice without being able to see his face made it that much sexier and daring. After settling on a video, I turned on my vibrator and tossed my head back against the pillow. Seconds before I climaxed to his hypnotizing baritone voice, Mav walked through the bedroom door. Startled and embarrassed, I quickly tossed the iPad to the ground and twisted my vibrator off.

"River, what the fuck were you doin' in here?" he asked.

Still stunned, I replied, "I was just—nothing. I wasn't doing anything."

"You were playin' with your pussy without me. Why you couldn't wait for me to get home?"

I shrugged. "You were taking too long."

"You could've called. I would've found a way to get here if you needed me, baby."

"It's not that deep, Mav. There was no emergency. I'm fine and so is Noemi. My body just misses you, that's all."

"So, you went and started listenin' to that black ass nigga, again?"

I chuckled while rolling my eyes. "You know about that?"

"I've heard you before in the bathroom, and you had

me ready to bust in there on more than one occasion about to fuck his ass up until I realized it was some fetish shit you into." He chuckled.

I sunk lower into the bed, embarrassed yet tickled. "Whatever. I think it's cute when you get jealous over a nigga whose face I've never even seen."

"It's the principal," he smirked, "did you at least finish?"

"No."

"Good," he said while pulling his shirt over his head.

I let my teeth sink into my bottom lip as I watched Mav undress right in front of me. Instead of saying anything, I turned the vibrator back on and spread my legs again. His dark brown eyes fastened on mine as a smile creased his face.

"That's it, baby. Play with that sweet ass pussy," he growled.

He walked over to the bed with a sly grin across his face and kneeled at my side. Instead of removing the toy, he let me finish until I was gripping the sheets with my eyes rolling back into my head. As soon as I climaxed, I locked my eyes on him and smiled with eagerness. His dick was the cure all for my stress and ailments, and I was long overdue for my next dose.

The fan whirred above us as he tossed the covers to the floor. He walked over to the dressed and pulled out a silk scarf to blindfold me with.

"What are you doing?" I asked.

"I want you to tell me who makes you cum harder. Me or that nigga," he said, tying the scarf over my eyes.

I flashed a devilish grin. "Okay."

"Lay on your back," he commanded.

I indulged him and laid parallel to the bed. Seconds later, I felt his lips wrapped around each of my toes, sucking them one by one.

"Oooh shit," I said coolly.

He kissed up my legs and licked up and down my inner thigh before pushing my legs up toward my forehead and started eating until he was full. Mav started by kissing my lower set of lips slowly and blowing his breath against my clit. I arched my back in pleasure as he flicked his longue tongue against my clit and tugged at my nipples.

Riding the wave, I began thrusting my kitten into his juicy lips. I wanted nothing more than to look down at him and see his juicy lips in between my thighs, face, and mouth as wet as the ocean as he slurped me up like a cat with warm milk.

"Give me the dick, baby. I need you, Mav," I whimpered. Saying his name felt smooth against my tongue.

"Mmm, you need me?" he whispered, lips brushing across my inner thigh.

"Yes, baby! I need you right now."

"You gotta cum first. I ain't gon' give you the dick until you cum on this tongue, River."

My body shook with pleasure. His words alone were enough to send me over the edge, springing me into ecstasy. "Ooooh fuckkkkkkkk," I moaned.

Cumming that hard made my whole body go weak, but he soon made it clear that we were nowhere near finished.

"Can I take this off now? I wanna see your face," I told him.

"You can."

I slowly slid the blindfold off my face and tossed it to the floor. Mav laid on his back, and I kissed down his bare chest while straddling him.

He sucked in air through his teeth as I slowly lowered myself down, putting him inside me for the first time in months. "Goddamn."

My nails scraped his skin as my pussy bobbed up and down on his dick, speeding up with every fleeting second. Mav pulled my lips onto his as he ran his fingers through my wild hair. "Mmm, fuck yeah."

I rode him harder and faster, bucking like a raging bronco. "I missed every inch of you," I said, pressing the palms of my hands into his chest as I bucked forward.

"I missed you too," he said, before pulling me off him and bending me over.

He wasted no time eating my pussy from behind. I winded my hips in slow circles against his face as I closed my eyes and enjoyed the feeling of him tongue-fucking me to my next climax. Mav sunk his teeth into my ass cheek before pushing into me from behind.

"Ahhhh shit!" I screamed, burying my face into the nearest pillow.

"You like it when I fuck you like this?" he asked.

"Yes, fuck me just like this, Mav! Yes, yes yessss!"

"Arch your back and bounce that mothafucka back on this dick," he demanded, before sliding a finger inside my ass.

That alone drove me wild. With my mouth gaped open, he gripping my hair and yanked my head back so that he could wrap his hand around my throat again.

Stick that tongue out for daddy," he commanded.

I sucked on his index and middle fingers, getting them wet. Then, he reached down to massage my clit with them.

"Who makes you cum harder?"

"You baby!"

"You sure?" he asked, thrusting deeper.

"Oh, my God! Yes, baby it's you. It's all you!"

Mav pulled my arms back like reigns on a horse as he pushed in deeper, galloping into me.

"It's soooo fuckin' deep!" I shouted.

"Huh? What you say? Daddy can't hear you."

"I said it's soooo fuckin' d—deep, baby!"

He continued stretching my walls, supplying hard, deep strokes. I reached around and spread my ass cheeks for him, craving every inch until he flipped me over onto my back.

With his hands enclosed around my throat, Mav slid his tongue inside my mouth. He teasingly slid his dick up and down my wetness and pressing against my slit before pushing back inside of me. He locked his arms underneath my legs, delivering one deep stroke after another.

"Fuckkkkkkkk! It's—it's soooo goooooood!" I screamed out, choking on my words at the same time.

I looked down at him between my legs as he slid his dick all the way out to the tip and then plunged back in deep. I could see the white cream on his dick from my cum.

"Mmm, that's what I wanted to see. Look how much of a mess you made on this dick," he said, flicking my sensitive clit with his thumb.

I screamed out in pleasure, making sure the heavens and everyone down the block knew his name. "Cum inside me, baby! I want to feel every drop."

Mav pumped harder, obliging my wishes. "Fucccck!" he roared.

"Yessss! Right there! Right there!"

"Ahhhh shit!"

He had officially doused the fire burning inside me

and filled me with his seed.

Moments after we finished, Mav's phone began to ring. Breathing heavily, he reached around on the floor for his jeans and answered. "Yeah? W—what?"

His body stiffened, and he fell silent. He slowly pulled the phone down from his ear. I reached out for him, and his body was hot to the touch. I crawled around to face him and look him in the eyes. He was staring at the wall in front of him breathing heavy and nostrils flaring.

"Who was that, Mav?"

"Mav? Who was on the phone?"

"What's wrong, baby?"

A silent tear rolled down his cheek, and he automatically swiped his hand down his face. "FUCKKKKKKKKK!" he roared.

"Mav, you're scaring me. Who was that? What did they say?"

"It's Sosa…he's dead…"

Mav

Nausea coursed through my stomach the second I heard the news that yet another person close to me was gone. My fists balled up in rage as I shot out of the room and down to my safe. With my gold-plated gun in hand, I made the one phone call I'd been waiting to make.

"I've been waiting on your call," Uncle Salt said when he answered.

"I needed to be sure."

"And did you find the answers you sought out to find?"

"Yeah, and I need soldiers. This mothafucka dies

tonight."

"Say less, nephew."

When I hung up, I looked up to see River standing in the door frame. "Just promise me you'll make it back in one piece...okay? Noemi needs you...we both do," she said, making no attempt to change my mind.

"And if I don't, you know what to do. Take Noemi, the passports, and get the fuck outta the city, River."

She nodded while swiping a tear away from her cheek. "Okay, I will."

I tucked the gun in the back of my jeans and embraced her. "I love you."

She pressed her lips together and tightened her grip around my waist. "I love you so much, Mav."

"Now let me go. I gotta go." I pried her arms from around me and walked past her with devoid of emotion in my heart. I'd vowed to protect them from enemies known and unknown, and I was going to honor that.

THE ONE PHONE CALL I'd made landed Sebastian Keyes in my presence within the hour. Niggas ran down on him at a gas station near the airport and found a few packed bags in his backseat as if he was trying to skate out of town. It didn't matter where he ran, I was going to find his ass. They brought him to an undisclosed location where he'd be meeting with me one-on-one. I was going to remind him that I was a Malone and there wasn't a trace of bitch in my DNA. Once he was tied up, I ripped the blindfold off his face.

"You had niggas kidnap me? If you wanted to meet with me, all you had to do was ask," he said, as soon as he looked up and saw me hovering over him.

"It took me a minute, but now I know for sure. This you?" I asked, pulling out Suki's phone and playing the voicemails.

"I would give you a round of applause for figuring it out, but I'm a little tied up at the moment," he retorted as if I wouldn't splatter his brains within seconds.

"I trust you made good on your promise and took care of Lauren now that you didn't get your money. I mean, you wouldn't live up to your last name if you didn't make good on your word, right?" he asked.

"You seem to know a lot about me and the way my family does business, now let me tell you what I know about you," I said, aiming my gun at his head.

"You don't know shit about me!"

"Oh, is that right, *Nathaniel*?"

"W—what?"

"Or should I say, *Agent* Nathaniel Ferguson. Is that

better?" I clarified.

His eyes bulged. "W—what? I don't know what the fuck you're talking about, nigga. I ain't no cop."

"Oh, I know you ain't no cop. You're a mothafuckin' DEA agent!" I roared.

Fear suddenly left his eyes as a smile widened across his face. "I guess you are smarter than you look."

Sosa had looked out before he died. When I asked him to look into him and find out whatever he could, he did just that. He gave me information on him, and I held onto it, knowing I'd need it to come out on top. After I made the phone call to my uncle, I started looking into everything on the flash drive that Sosa had given me. Finding out he was undercover was something I didn't expect.

"What makes you think I don't have DEA enforcement officers swarming the building right fuckin' now, huh?"

"7829 Maple Leaf Street, Charlotte, North Carolina," I replied.

He frowned. "What the fuck? How did you find that?"

"That's your mother's address, right? Because I've got hittas parked outside her spot right now ready and waiting for me to say the word."

He scoffed. "It seems like you've thought of everything."

He was nothing but a dirty undercover DEA agent who'd gotten caught up in his lies to decipher reality from fiction. He'd been put into the field over two years ago to try and take my family's entire operation down. He seemingly went off the grid for a while and came back as Sebastian Keyes, a real estate investor with money for days, until he met Suki and it all dried up.

"You must've really enjoyed pretending to be somebody you're not, huh? I guess until Suki robbed you."

"Fuck her! I loved her, and she tried to kill me!"

"And when she didn't succeed, you went after her and my brother!"

"She took everything from me! The bitch deserved everything she got. I could've saved her, but she didn't want to be saved."

I scoffed. "You let a bitch play you, and you took my blood from me in the process. The only thing I want to know is why us? What the fuck did my family ever do to you for you to go so fuckin' hard to tear us down?"

"Why not you? Have you seen first-hand what your

drugs do to communities? What you do to households? You don't give a fuck whose lives you tear apart as long as the money's right, right? Is that it? You don't give a fuck! None of you ever do! So, I made it my goal to take your family's entire operation down. I'm the good guy in this scenario, Malone, not you!"

I refused to have a pissing match with him about the levels of good and evil to prove which one of us was better than the other. Nor was I going to glorify what my family did. We both had blood on our hands, at the end of the day, and we would never see eye-to-eye because we were on opposite ends of the law. I wasn't into killing law enforcement, but there was no mercy for enemies, whether they wore a badge or not. He had a vendetta against my entire family, and he'd taken too much from me. His ass had to be dealt with.

The next sound he heard was my gun cocking. "So this is it, huh? And what happens after they find my body? Back to the cell you go! And I hope you fuckin' rot!"

"Don't worry, they'll never fuckin' find your body," I assured him just before I lit his body up like the Fourth of July.

I watched as blood reddened the ground he laid on and didn't move until I heard each one of the shells hit the ground. Justice had finally been served. As soon as I was certain he'd taken his final breath, I called in my Uncle Salt's men and had them take care of the cleanup. I changed my clothes and burned them before wiping the prints off Suki's phone, sealing it up and dropping it off in my lawyer's overnight box. Little did he know, I'd just hand delivered the key to my freedom. Everything he needed to prove my innocence was there, connecting the nigga I'd just killed to the deaths of my brother and Suki. After getting back in my car, I whipped out my phone to text him my instructions.

Me: [2:48 a.m.]: *Proof of my innocence is in your overnight box. Take it down to the police department and all this should go away.*

"Checkmate," I said, before pulling off.

Now that I'd completed what I'd set out to do, I felt myself reflecting on my actions and what Noemi would think of me if she knew all the things I'd done just to avenge her father. Had it not been the fact that I'd fallen completely in love with Noemi, I would've let Suki's parents take her. Knowing what I knew about her mother, I would be a fool to allow her to grow up and be anything like her. As far as I was concerned, I was Noemi's saving grace. She was better off with me.

I was still grappling with the fact that I'd led Sosa straight into the lion's den. I knew better than anybody that casualties were just as much as part of the war as the victory, but I missed him and had to make sure his family and kids were taken care of. My thoughts led me to the cemetery where Luca and Suki's bodies had been laid to rest.

I shook my head while staring at the words written on his headstone, *Beloved husband, father, and brother.* He was so much more than that.

"It's done, my nigga. You can rest easy now," I assured him, "and don't worry about Noemi. I got her for life. She'll never want for anything.

I took a seat and rested my back against the cold stone. "Yo, you remember when I first got out and you told me that one day I was gon' meet my match, and she was gon' have me eatin' out the palm of her hand and shit? Well, you were right. I got River's ass and shit, she got my ass too. She's been great with Noemi. If it wasn't for her, I don't know where I'd be. I'ma have to fuck around and take a page out of your book one day and get down on one knee or somethin'." I chuckled.

I kept talking even though I knew I'd never get the response I craved. Yet, it felt so comforting just to let it all out. I'd never properly grieved his death. I just kept putting all of my grief into finding out who'd taken him from me.

I wiped a single tear from my face. "I fuckin' miss you every day, nigga. With me just getting out after already missing out on five years of your life, I just—I wasn't ready to say goodbye, you know? I'm sorry for the shit I said that night and I wasn't there for you when you needed me the most. I'm sorry, I couldn't protect you from Suki and all of her bullshit."

I lowered my head, knowing that even though it wasn't my fault, I'd carry the grief around and probably never fully forgive myself for not being my brother's keeper in his time of need. The silence of the night took over, and I sat quietly with my thoughts for a few minutes before pulling myself back up on my feet.

"It's all love, Luca. You and Sosa rest easy up there, and save a spot for a nigga," I said, nodding my head up to the sky.

I walked away, knowing my brother could finally rest in peace. Any secrets that I didn't know about him or Suki, would stay buried with them. I was going to keep my promise to Luca and continue to raise Noemi as if she was my own. That meant I had to do better and be better for her no matter what. It wasn't until then that I understood why our father fought so hard to keep us away from the streets and show us what living a legit life looked like. Noemi deserved that and so much more.

River

I woke up to the sound of water running in the bathroom sink. The bathroom light was shining underneath the door, and I could hear Mav fumbling around inside. I tip-toed out of bed and walked into the bathroom to see a shirtless Mav hovered over the sink. Drops of blood splattered into the sink as he rinsed out his mouth. We stood in silence, talking only with our eyes for a few seconds as we stared at each other's reflection in the mirror. I gave him a once over, taking in the bruises on his ribs and scratches on his face.

"It's done," he finally spoke up.

I nodded. "Are you—"

"Yes, I'm okay," he replied before I could even finish my sentence.

"Good." I nodded again.

I walked up behind him and wrapped my arms around his waist. "Seeing that side of you scares me."

"I don't want you to be scared of me."

"You promised me this would be the end, and I just need to know that you're sure about it…because the anxiety I feel every time you walk out of that door, I can't keep feeling that Mav."

"I'm done. You have my word, I'm all yours."

All I could do was hope and pray that things would settle back into normalcy for us. We needed peace to wash over the entire household. Noemi deserved it, and so did we.

One month later.

The day for Noemi's sixth birthday party had finally come, and although it was nowhere near as elaborate and fancy as the five parties before it, it was done in love and that was all that mattered.

Happy birthday to you.

Happy birthday to you.

Happy birthday, dear Noemi.

Happy birthday to you.

After all the candles had been blown out, presents had been opened and guests finally started to trickle out. Mav and I were cleaning up when I stopped to yawn.

"You tired as hell, huh?" he asked.

"Today was the longest day ever. I feel like I can barely keep my eyes open."

"Go ahead and get in the shower and then get in the bed. I got the rest, and whatever I don't get, it'll be cleaned up tomorrow."

I nodded before another yawn escaped from my mouth. "Yeah, I think I might take you up on that offer."

"You sure you, okay? Besides tired, you've been lookin' bothered all day."

"Have I?" I asked.

I don't know why I was surprised that he could see right through me. He'd always been able to.

"Stop fuckin' around with me, River. What's on

your mind?"

"Well, I do have something to tell you, but I'm scared to even say it out loud," I confessed.

"Is it going to make me mad?" he asked, putting down the trash bag in his hand.

I shrugged. "I hope not."

"What is it?"

"I took a test a couple days ago," I said, while sliding my hands in my back pockets.

"What kind of test?"

"One where the stick turns pink or blue…"

He shot his eyes over at me. "You took a pregnancy test?"

I nodded. "Yeah…"

"And?"

"I'm pregnant, Mav. We might be having a baby…"

"Might be? Are you pregnant or not?"

"I am, I mean at least that's what the three tests that I took said, I just… you know, I don't want to get my hopes up."

He shook his head. "Nah, fuck that. Get 'em up. Get 'em all the way up. You gon' have my baby, River. If it's meant to be, it'll happen. But regardless, I got you every step of the way," he assured me.

"How can you be so…I don't know, sure about any of this?"

"I'm not, but I know that I wouldn't want to be having this conversation with anyone else but you. We gon' be good, regardless."

I smiled and wrapped my arms around him. "Thank you, baby. I really needed to hear that."

"I love you, River," he said, gently grazing his hand across my stomach, "and I love you too, little one."

I felt relieved to get the news off my chest and even more relieved to know that I had someone who would stand by me no matter what came our way. For the first time in a long time, it felt like we were finally going to get our shot at a true happily ever after.

Mav

To me, no other woman could even come close to River. Everything about her may not have been perfect, but she was perfect for me. There was no doubt in my mind that I'd fallen in love for the first and last time. Finding out that she was pregnant was unnerving and exciting all at the same time. I was nervous about becoming more than just a father figure to someone because I knew the weight and the consequences my previous lifestyle and my last name carried, but I was prepared to take on the job. If she was going to be the mother of my child, it was only right that I made it official and asked her to become my wife. I'd had the ring for a few weeks and was just waiting for the perfect time to present itself.

River turned back to look at me and saw me staring at her. "What?" she mumbled.

"Marry me," I told her.

"What? What did you just say?" she asked.

"I said, marry me, River."

She reached out and grabbed the sides of my face. "Mav, are you serious?"

"I've never been more serious," I said as I presented her with a black ring box.

"Mav… are you fuckin' serious?" she asked with

tears in her eyes.

"Why don't you open the box and see for yourself?"

River quickly took the box from me and popped it open. Settled inside was an eighteen-karat gold halo-cut diamond ring. She placed her hand over her mouth as tears slid down the sides of her cheeks.

"Oh, my God." She trembled.

I took the ring out of the box and slid it on her ring finger. She held her hand up and admired the ring as she turned her hand from left to right.

"Is that a yes?" I asked.

River nodded as she threw her arms around my neck and started kissing my face.

"Yes! Of course, it's a yes!"

"I love you, River."

"I love you more, baby! I love you so much more!"

Epilogue

8 ½ months later

River

I could feel my heartbeat ringing in my ears, thudding louder and louder. The only thing that could drown it out was the sound of my own screams. Throughout my entire pregnancy, I was determined that I wouldn't take any medication just because I was already high risk, but the more intense the pain got, the quicker I started to recant my decision. My contractions were kicking my ass double-time. It definitely wasn't anything I'd prepared myself for. The nurses had set me up in a room and strapped me to a heart monitor. By that time, I was shaking like a leaf on a tree. All I wanted to do was have a successful, natural delivery. Every time a new contraction surged, Mav would count with me slowly as I tried to focus on my breathing. It was almost natural for me to hold my breath through the pain, but the nurses kept having to remind me to exhale and take deep breaths.

By the time the doctors were ready for me to push, I was already both mentally and physically exhausted. My hair was in a lopsided half bun on top of my head with loose ringlets hanging from the back and the sides and sticking to my sweaty skin. It had taken thirteen and a half hours for me to dilate to ten centimeters. All I wanted was for someone to base up my vagina like a turkey and slide my baby out while I slept through it all.

"Okay, River. I want you to give me another big push on the count of three, okay? One… two… push," my doctor coached.

With my chin nestled into my chest, I pushed down as hard as I could, and my baby's head finally began to crown.

"That's it, River! Give me one more big, hard push and hold it until I count to ten, okay?"

I clenched Mav's hand as tight as I could while curling my toes. As exhausted as I was, I was prepared to give it one last try.

"On three, okay? One—two—three!"

"Mmmm ahhhhhhhh!" I screamed with my eyes slammed shut and my chin pressed into my chest.

"That's it, Mama! You're doing it! You're about to bring your baby into this world!" the nurse holding my leg cheered.

The moment I drew in my next breath of air, the room was filled with the melodic screams of my newborn baby. My eyes opened slowly, and I squinted as colorful circles danced in front of me. All of a sudden, the room had gotten brighter than I'd remembered. The nurses wiped the baby down before placing him on my thudding chest. As soon as I held him in my arms, and he heard the sound of my voice, he started to settle down. Just looking into his precious brown eyes for the first time made me want to cry. The feeling was indescribable. I was just so thankful to have a healthy baby boy. I vowed that I was never going to let any harm come his way. He was my little prince, Noemi was my princess, and Maverick was the king of my heart. Together, the four of us were the family that I never thought I'd have. Maverick Muhammad Malone, Jr. weighed seven pounds and six ounces and was twenty-two inches long. He had lungs of steel the way he pushed out his first cry while in my arms and a full head of jet-black hair.

"He's here. You did it," Mav said, never taking his eyes off his first-born son.

I was filled to the brim with emotion. Excitement. Nerves. Sadness. Joy. Each different, but all taking up identical amounts of space in my brain. After finding out it would be difficult for me to get pregnant, let alone carry to full-term, becoming a mother was something I'd written off for myself. As long as I had Noemi, I convinced myself I would be fine. The moment I found out I was pregnant again, everything changed. Mav's excitement to become a father to his own seed was infectious, and I began to picture what life would look like with two kids to raise. It brought my heart joy to be able to give him a family and a legacy of his own.

"He's so beautiful," I said, gently tapping his nose.

"I think he looks just like you. He's got your eyes and nose," Mav told me.

I tilted my head to the side. "Are you sure? I can't see it. When I look at him, all I see is you."

Mav leaned in to kiss my forehead. "Thank you, baby."

"For what?"

"For giving me something no other woman could ever give me; my first-born son, and my heart in human form."

Tears quickly flooded my eyes. Who would've ever

thought I'd find my dream man in someone that I once loathed? Before Maverick, I'd never even considered dating a man who sold drugs or lived the street life, let alone fall in love with him the way I did. It's true what they say, love will make you do some crazy things. Our relationship had been stained with pending prison sentences, long, sleepless nights, secrets, and more legal drama than either of us ever anticipated. Yet, the bond the two of us shared had proven itself to be unbreakable. Never in a million years did I think fatherhood and a relationship would look so good on him. Together, Noemi, Mav, and I had become a family. Adding our son only made our family that much more complete. Nothing was ever going to break us apart.

The End

a note from k.l. hall.

Reader,

Thank you for reading the finale of *The Illest Taboo* series. Please, if you've made it this far, I hope you'll consider taking a minute to tell me what you thought about the book in the form of a **book review and/or rating**. Don't hesitate to let me know what you'd like to see from me next! I thoroughly enjoy reading your reviews and hearing from you as well! I'm always striving to attract new readers and retain current ones, and reviews are one of the easiest ways to attract readers. If you loved the book, tell a friend, and most importantly let me know!

k.l. hall

P.S. I created a special playlist just for this book. Check it out by clicking here. (E-Book Only)

about the author.

As a serial storyteller, K.L. Hall pens enthralling love stories intertwined with the grittiness of urban fiction. Her writing style is a fusion of eminently relatable female characters like Sydney Tate and Raquel Valentine, and the flawed, yet desirable male leads who love them, like Law Calloway and Justice Silva.

Reader Faves:
In the Arms of a Savage: (Peaked at #1 in Women's Fiction)
As Long as You Stay Down: (Peaked at #2 in African American Erotica)
Awakened: A Paranormal Romance: (Peaked at #1 in Erotic Science Fiction)

Sign up for my mailing list to stay up to date with new releases, giveaways, sneak peeks, and more! Click this link: https://bit.ly/38RMpV5 *(E-Book Only)*

Connect with me on social media:

Facebook: https://www.facebook.com/authorklhall

Twitter: https://twitter.com/authorklhall

Instagram:
https://www.instagram.com/officialklhall/

Website: https://www.authorklhall.com

Other novels by K.L. Hall:

Diary of a Hood Princess 1-3

Rise of a Street King: The Justice Silva Story *(Spin-Off to the Diary of a Hood Princess series)*

Where He Belongs: A Disrespectful Love Story

Love Me Harder: A Sin City Love Story

Broken Condoms and Promises 1-3

In the Arms of a Savage 1-3

Built for a Savage: Blaze and Camille's Love Story *(Spin-Off to the In the Arms of a Savage Series)*

A Ruthle$$ Love Story 1-3

Fallin' for the Alpha of the Streets 1-2

The Most Savage of Them All: The Wolfe Calloway Story *(Prequel to the In the Arms of a Savage*

Series)

When a Gangsta Loves a Good Girl

Caught Between my Husband and a Hustler

The Illest Taboo 1-2

Novellas:

Bi-Curious: An Erotic Tale

Bi-Curious 2: Tastes Like Candy

House of Cards 1-2

A Savage Calloway Christmas *(Christmas novella to the In the Arms of a Savage Series)*

Lovin' the Alpha of the Streets: A Valentine's Day Novella *(Valentine's Day novella to the Fallin' for the Alpha of the Streets Series)*

Awakened: A Paranormal Romance

As Long as You Stay Down

Children's Books:

Princess for Hire

Princess Twinkle Toes & the Missing Magic Sneakers

Little One, Change the World

Adjust Your Crown: A Self-Love Coloring Book for Children of Color

Non-Fiction:

Authors are a Business: The Booked & Busy Course Mini Book

CPSIA information can be obtained
at www.ICGtesting.com
Printed in the USA
LVHW082345030921
696898LV00013B/420